THE COWBOY

THE KING FAMILY SAGA BOOK 4

MOLLY O'KEEFE

To YOU! The Keepers and the readers. To the BBRL crowd and the Racy Readers. To my library readers and my review crew. To my readers - I can not thank you enough.

B EA

EVERY MORNING WAS a 6:30 wake-up call.

Didn't matter when I went to bed, because Thelma and Louise simply did not care about me and beauty sleep. It started at about 6:25 with Thelma nudging my leg with her nose. And a nudge from a 130-pound mastiff was more like a shove. If I didn't move fast enough after that Louise got into it and the Chihuahua wasn't subtle. By 6:30 she was on the bed, making herself comfortable—right across my face.

"I'm up. I'm up," I muttered, pushing Louise off my head. I gave her a little scratch as she went. "It's a good thing you're cute."

When I sat up, my legs over the side of the mattress, Thelma put her front paws on my knees and bathed my face with her sticky dog tongue. "Okay, okay. You're cute, too. You're both very cute."

They weren't. Unless it was in the They're So Ugly They're Cute category, in which case...maybe.

"Come on." I pushed her off. But I gave her a little chin rub as I did it.

I slipped my feet into my flip-flops and shoved my hair out of my face. The apartment I rented above a storefront was at the far end of Main Street. On one side of the building was The Bar. The only bar with actual seats in Dusty Creek, which only barely made it the best. On the other side of my apartment was a heavily forested ravine, at the bottom of which was the creek the town was named after.

Not at all dusty, so I'm not sure why it got that name.

Anyway, I checked to see if I had pants on because I'd made that mistake once or three hundred times when I took the dogs out. This morning I did not, in fact, have pants on, but my shirt was plenty long. So I went down the narrow stairs that led to the side door and the dogs raced out into the ravine where they went to the bathroom.

"Be quick," I told them. Which they usually were. Sometimes Thelma would get distracted by a squirrel but the promise of breakfast kept her on task.

"Morning," my sister Sabrina called out as she walked over from her bakery, Sweet Things, across the street. Sweet Things was cute and her cupcakes were delicious, but I didn't tell her that. The only reason I didn't curl my lip and hiss at her as she crossed the street was that she was bringing me a cup of coffee. She'd started doing this lately. Bringing me coffee when she saw me out here from the big front window of her bakery.

Ronnie had asked her to do it. To be nice to me—nicer, anyway. Just like she asked me to give Sabrina a chance. To *try*.

These coffee dates were us...trying.

They were *awful*.

"Hey," I said. She handed me the mug and took a sip from hers. Both of us looked at the ravine like it was interesting. I wondered if she was hoping it might spontaneously burst into flames so we wouldn't have to make our awkward small talk.

Because I sure as hell was.

"Air smells good," I said, taking a big sniff of it. "What are you making?"

"Chocolate cakes."

"That'll do it. You're covered in flour," I said.

"It's my new look."

"It's in your hair."

She put her hand to that high bouncy ponytail, giving it a shake. Sabrina used to be a reality TV star, one of the most beautiful people in the world—all the magazines said so. And she looked completely different than she used to. Looser, happier, less rigidly perfect. So different you wouldn't even recognize her.

A few weeks ago I told her she was prettier now than she ever was before.

Which you wouldn't think would cause a fight. But you would be wrong.

"Clayton and Ronnie are coming out to the ranch at the end of the month for dinner." She was very carefully not looking at me.

"Sounds nice." It sounded like having all my skin stripped off and being dipped in alcohol. Surrounded by my sisters and their husbands and all their love?

No thanks.

"You could come?"

"Is that an invite?"

She sucked a deep breath through her nose. "I'd love you to come. You could bring a date."

"I don't have a date."

"Bea King without a date?" She shot me a laughing look over the edge of her mug.

I held my arms out wide. "No date."

No date in over year. Since Travis. Since Ronnie fell in love. Since Dad died and our lives fell apart. I hadn't so much as sniffed a man in a year.

"I'm taking a break from being Bea King," I said.

"Yeah? How is that working?"

"Great," I snapped. "Just great."

Frankly, it was nice not being me. The fuck-up. The King most likely to fail. It was nice not needing Ronnie to bail me out.

But sometimes it felt like I was going to twitch out of my skin. Sometimes it felt like I wanted to pull every fire alarm in town. Start a fight on Main Street just to...relieve this feeling in me. This pressure.

This awful, awful boredom.

The sense of not being myself. Of having lost myself when I tried to make everything right.

"Bea," she said, and that tone of her voice, that *let's be friends so you can tell me all your problems and then I'll mock you mercilessly for them* tone. Yeah, I wasn't here for that tone. For the sisterly love.

I had one sister for that.

"Thanks." I cut her off. "For the coffee."

"No problem." Ugh. Her smile was the fake one I recognized from her television show.

"You don't have to do it, you know," I said.

"Yeah," she said. "I know."

See, this was Sabrina and me. A nice gesture could lead

to a fight with one left turn.

"I'm just saying I appreciate it."

"Yeah. I can tell. Bring me the mug later." And then she was gone. Back across the street. She had two white flour handprints on the butt of her cutoffs.

The apology that would make so much of this go away, the apology that might actually start the two of us being friends, was right on the edge of my lips. But I didn't say it.

I couldn't give her the satisfaction. Because she never gave me the satisfaction.

And that was pure Bea King.

There was a giant crash just on the other side of the wall behind me. I jumped and sloshed coffee all over the place, and then there was another. A thud, a crumble, silence, and then repeat. Steadily. Over and over again. Dust rained down from the ceiling of the vestibule.

Shit. The demo work. Jack had told me about that. He'd bought the building where I lived with plans to take over the first floor and expand The Bar's dining space. He gave me a discount on the rent because I was basically going to be living over a construction zone.

Demo was starting today. And, apparently, at dawn. I should probably get grumpy about that, but I couldn't really manage it. I could sleep through anything but the dog's routine. But the noise would probably stir Thelma and Louise up earlier and earlier.

It really was time for a new place, and I needed to get serious about looking. This ravine was keeping things manageable for now, but I couldn't keep a Chihuahua and a mastiff in a two-room apartment forever.

You know you're rich. That's what my sister Ronnie had said the last time she visited me here. Looking around at my secondhand furniture with her nose wrinkled. A portion of the inheritance that my Dad left us had been divvied up and after paying off all my debt and the money my sister had loaned me—with interest—after the Travis debacle, I had roughly three-and-a-half million dollars in my bank account. With the promise of more to come.

More.

It was already more money than I knew what to do with. So much money, in fact, that I was kind of terrified of it. It was giving me anxiety. Me! Bea King, the rebel child. The guaranteed good time.

I was not supposed to have anxiety, but this money was giving it to me.

It was a life-changing amount of money and I was determined not to waste it. I just needed to figure out what I wanted my life to be before I spent anything on it.

And that was a harder question than I'd thought. Or maybe it was the answer that was hard. Whichever. I couldn't make a decision. That money had been in my account for three months and all I'd done was buy a used Jeep, rent a cheap apartment, and buy my dogs really good dog food.

Ronnie wanted me to go back to school, which, sure... made sense. I didn't have a degree. Degrees were useful. But a degree in what?

Sabrina said I needed to travel. See the world. Get some perspective, those were her words. But I think she just wanted me out of town.

In the aftermath of my Dad dying, both my sisters found the things that made them happy.

Why the hell couldn't I?

What was wrong with me?

I tried to shake off this feeling but it lingered like a bad smell.

When the dogs came bounding up from the ravine we all went back upstairs where I filled their bowls with kibble and the dogs sat side by side next to the sliding glass door that led to the deck, pretending they were well behaved.

"You're not fooling anyone, you know," I told them.

I wondered if *I* was. Fooling anyone. This new, not Bea, Bea.

The door let in plenty of light and the deck was literally in the middle of all those trees. It felt like the most private, secluded placed in the world. I'd put some privacy fencing along the side of the deck that faced the street, because sometimes a girl liked to sit in the sun with her top off, you know?

And my backyard was dominated by a giant Texas live oak. It was a beauty. Had to be hundreds of years old, with branches that absolutely filled the blue sky with green leaves. It was covered in all kinds of moss.

The tree was so big I couldn't get my arms around it. Two of me probably couldn't get our arms around it. And the branches dipped, some close to the ground, before rising up to the sky. Every time there was a good storm I worried that part of that tree was going to take down my little deck.

But it was rock solid, that tree.

And it was easily the best privacy screen ever made.

Between it and the fence I could do naked yoga out there and no one would ever know it.

I should do more yoga. Would yoga help me make a decision? Would yoga make me happy?

"Hold on to your boobs," I told the girls, who whined at me to hurry up and get their breakfast. I set the dog bowls on the counter, opened the door, and all but threw the bowls down on the concrete pad of my second-floor deck. I went back in for my cup of coffee and the dogs went after the food like it might run away from them.

It was why I fed them out here. It was a full top-to-bottom kitchen cleanup when I fed them indoors.

I had a little planter stand filled with flowers I was trying to kill with my attention and love. I drank my coffee and picked off all the dead blooms.

And when the dogs went indoors I bent down to get the bowls, but then decided, what the hell, and tried to press my hands flat to the ground. The breeze came up behind me and pushed my shirt up over my ass.

Yoga.

"Sorry...I just...you're not alone out here."

I stood up and realized over the spindles of my wrought-iron railing I could see parts of a man through the leaves of the oak tree in the back corner of the yard, where he seemed to be making a pile of debris.

"I'm almost done," he said, and tossed an armful of wood onto the pile. "And you can go back to...you know."

Bending over without pants on. Right.

"You can see me?"

"Parts of you."

"What parts?"

His laugh was low and dark, and I could see he wore blue jeans and a sweaty T-shirt. I couldn't see his face. But that arm was strong. And he had a nice laugh.

"Well, if you don't mind me saying. I can see the good parts."

Yeah, I bet you can cowboy. He lifted his hat off his head and ran a hand through his hair, which I couldn't see. But I could see that forearm. Tan from the sun. Corded from hard work. There were flecks of sawdust stuck in the sweat.

It was a very nice forearm attached to a thick, strong wrist. With a big hand at the end.

A man's hand.

My skin itched and my body twitched and I felt that recklessness roll right through me. Which was the only reason—well, that and the small connected muscles in his forearm—that I said, "Yeah, I can see the good parts, too."

He went really still and I had the rarely felt sensation of having gone too far. A step over the line. I'd shocked my polite cowboy with jacked forearms. Well, I was out of the business of apologizing or trying to make a man comfortable with who I was.

A losing proposition every time.

So I turned my back to him and bent back over. I had to bend my knees to get my hands on the floor but I did it. Aware all the time of how my ass must look in the red silk underwear I wore.

Good. My ass was fucking top-notch. He was the luckiest cowboy in Dusty Creek to be getting this show from Bea King.

You don't like it cowboy, you can leave.

He didn't. Of course he didn't.

I stood back up, nice and slow, laughing a little in my throat, because this was a surprisingly good time.

"You're the guy working downstairs?"

"Yeah, sorry if I woke you."

"You by yourself?"

"Yeah…it's just me."

I hummed like I was considering something and he was just going to have to wait to find out what it was.

"I'm not—"

"Don't talk," I said. Because if I knew him, or he knew

me, this shit would get ruined fast. And I just wanted a few more minutes.

He cleared his throat instead of saying anything. Smart guy, he caught on fast. He was just lucky to have seen me. That was all. Lucky enough to have looked up and found me on my deck.

He could be anyone. He could be a prince. A hit man. A construction worker with a dirty, dirty mind. He could be dangerous. A really dangerous guy with dangerous plans. He could see me up here and decide he had to have me.

I could be anyone. A stripper working my way through college. The wife of an abusive man who kept me locked up here so I'd never leave him for another man.

I could be the kind of person people counted on and I came through for them.

I could be happy.

Something like grief tore through me. Something strange and painful and I wanted it to go away. A million years ago, when I was Bea King, I'd get drunk or start a fight. I'd pick a handsome cowboy out of the crowd and let him fuck me until I could be happy again. Just for a few minutes.

But all that was behind me and I needed something else.

Teasing this cowboy might work. Might be just the thing. For a minute or two.

My nipples got hard under my shirt. Between my legs there was a buzzing that I liked. I liked it very much. This... what I was thinking...was ridiculous. And dangerous.

And that was why I liked it. Wanted it.

The silence in the backyard was charged and wild. I was charged and wild as I sat in the deck chair where I liked to drink my morning coffee.

And I spread my legs open just a little bit.

From this angle I really couldn't see him much at all. His

hand. His hip in blue jeans. That fucking forearm. It was obscene that forearm, the way it rippled with muscle and narrowed down to the bones of his wrist. I could imagine grabbing onto that wrist with both hands while he did... whatever the fuck he wanted with that hand.

I wanted to ask him to take a step to the side so I could see him better, but this was good. Better. Fantasy, in my case, was always better than reality.

And he must have been able to see me because he didn't move. Not a muscle. And he cleared his throat again, like it was a signal.

Go ahead. I'm here.

It had been a lonely year and I wasn't ready to invite some stranger into my house. And I wasn't about to engage in some masturbatory dirty talk. But I liked the thrill his eyes gave me.

My big oak tree gave us the right amount of mystery. And privacy.

Voyeurism. Who knew?

The buzzing between my legs changed tones and got deeper. Brighter. I spread my legs wider and ran my hands up from my knees to the silk edge of my panties. I did it again and then again until finally I ran my thumb over the damp spot, hitting my clit on the way up.

I gasped and he groaned and I imagined he could see enough to get turned on. Or maybe he couldn't really see anything and just sound of my gasp was enough to make his forearm clench up like that.

Or maybe he saw my face and he knew exactly who I was, but he wasn't interested in my knowing him.

This was going to work just fine for both of us.

I slipped my fingers under the top of my panties because I liked the way that looked. Dirty and secret. Like I didn't know he was down there. But I didn't want to be seen. I was a teenager with my hands under my desk and he was a teacher who shouldn't have been looking.

My knuckles rubbed up against that wet spot and I could smell the musty-sweet scent of my arousal in the air.

Could he? Did he like it?

He still hadn't moved. That forearm of his was rock solid so I knew he didn't have his own junk out. He was just watching. Just waiting. To see what I would do.

I was a fucking queen, that's what I was. And he was some lowly soldier who could have his eyes taken out just for seeing me this way. But he risked it...because I was amazing.

Something about this turned my crank pretty hard and when my thumb hit my clit I saw sparks. It was like every blood vessel in my body was dilating past what I could stand. The orgasm was coming fast and it was going to be hard.

"Fuck," I breathed, stroking my thumb over my clit again, just the way I liked it. A little harder on the down-stroke. Faster. I bent my head, braced my foot against the railing. I watched the sweat drip down his arm and I stroked myself until I came so hard I saw stars against the back of my eyelids.

But when I opened my eyes and looked down, he wasn't there. I couldn't see him anywhere in the yard.

Suddenly cold and just a little embarrassed I closed my legs.

"Hello?" I called out.

And then he was back, he took a step to the side and I saw that forearm again, the navy-blue sleeve of his shirt hugging his biceps. His hat was in his hand and I saw some blond hair.

"You're...fucking beautiful," he said.

I laughed with the magnanimous humor a good orgasm could give a girl. "You want to tell me your name?" I asked.

He was quiet for a long time, and it was just the wind in the oak tree and the sound of my heavy breathing. I wondered what secret he was keeping and why he wanted it kept. But frankly I wasn't interested in telling him my name, either. Nothing like the name King in this town to ruin a flirtation. Shit got weird when boys found out they might be able to fuck a King.

"No names," he said. "No faces. No talking. I'll be back here tomorrow morning."

And then my cowboy voyeur was gone.

2

B EA

THE BAR'S actual bar from end to end was roughly twenty feet by four feet. It was beat-up mahogany and the hard wood was soft and gray in places. The soda gun was mostly clogged and the ice machine worked intermittently.

And five days a week for the lunch and happy-hour shifts, I was the only one back there.

Which made me queen.

Queen of the worst shift in a dive bar in a nowhere town in East Texas.

And I honest to god loved it. That twenty feet for roughly six hours Wednesday to Sunday was the only place I wanted to be.

Jack's bar was pure dive bar. Nothing but fried food and beer coolers full of Abita and Shiner. The nicest thing we stocked was a California Pinot Grigio for the entirety of the white wine drinking public—namely, Sabrina. It's how I was being nice to her, having that wine and dramatically over-charging her for it.

I wasn't very good at being nice to her.

There was a Kentucky bourbon that I'd introduced Jack to. Sometimes after my shift on Friday afternoons I made us manhattans and we sat at the bar like Don Draper and gave Kimmy behind the bar a hard time.

Which—for those keeping track—also happened to be the extent of my social life.

It was the end of a quiet shift on Wednesday, which was a good thing because I was constantly talking myself out of asking Jack questions about the demo guy he'd hired for next door.

I had a hard time keeping my mouth shut on my best days, today the effort felt superhuman.

You're so fucking beautiful. He said that to me; he'd been real and not a figment of my imagination.

And I am not going to ask Jack about him. No names. That was his deal.

I wiped the last of the glasses and made sure everything was stocked for the night shift. Cherries for the bourbon sours I showed Kimmy how to make (with regular bourbon —not my good stuff). A cold bottle of Pinot Grigio in case Sabrina and Garrett came in for their weekly date night.

And—because it was Texas in the middle of summer— enough beer to put down the beer drinkers of Dusty Creek.

All in all, I was leaving Jack's bar better than when I found it. The night crew worked late and left the place in ruins. But I kind of liked that part of the job, too. Cleaning up, putting things to rights. After a lifetime of messing shit up, it was fun being on this end of it.

Jack sat at the end of the bar, nursing a cup of strong

coffee and cutting checks. He did this every Wednesday, and every Wednesday I lingered, waiting for my pay. He was a handsome guy, with dark hair that he wore just on the right side of too shaggy and dark eyes. A sarcastic grin that could take his face from little boy to serious man in point-five seconds. He'd opened The Bar a few years ago and he took it seriously.

"This is ridiculous, you know?" he said.

"Which part?" I asked.

"You waiting for a paycheck for..." he glanced at the amount on the check. "Three hundred bucks."

"Three hundred bucks is real money, Jack."

"You're a King, Bea. You have more money than God."

I had more money than God, one third of a giant spread just west of town, and a top-drawer stable of horses. The only thing I did to deserve it was get born a King.

Which wasn't a recommendation for anything.

"No. I'll have the tips I've made and three hundred bucks when you give me that check." He sighed and handed me the check. But then didn't let go of it.

I rolled my eyes at him.

"If you're hell bound to pretend you're not a King for a while, you know you'd make more money working at night," he said, for roughly the eight-hundredth time.

It had been years since I lived in this town and I didn't advertise that I was back, other than working at the bar. But everyone had long memories around here.

At night and on the weekends, there were too many people. Too much gossip and sideways glances. Too many assholes who hated my daddy who wanted to get a dig in on his daughter.

No thanks.

"I'm making good money working lunch and happy hour."

Now it was his turn to roll his eyes at me. Jack was a good guy. As far as bosses went he was easily in the top five I'd ever had. "I'm trying to give you a promotion," he said. "With the addition next door I'm going to need help. Real help. You have more experience running restaurants and bars than I do. You could manage—"

"For the hundredth time, I don't want to manage shit," I said and tugged on the check. Again, he didn't let go. "You're ruining my good mood, Jack."

"Don't want to manage? Or don't think you can do it? Because—"

"Jack," I said. "We've been over this. I am excellent at exceeding expectations only when they're set really low. Expect more from me and I will fail you. And I like you. I'm not interested in failing you."

"It's a bar, Bea. It's the same fucking bar you manage during the day. Like a fucking boss, I might add. Why do you think you're going to fail me?"

Because it was what I did. It was my one true skill.

I was a fuck-up. Ask anyone. Ask my sisters. Old boyfriends. My father if he wasn't already dead. Trust me with something and I would ruin it. It was my own very special gift.

"I need to get home to the dogs." This time when I tugged on the check hard enough to threaten ripping it, Jack let go.

"I don't know how you're surviving in that tiny apartment with those animals of yours."

No lie, Thelma, the mastiff, made it tricky. But it was Louise, the Chihuahua, who was making it impossible.

Jesus, I thought. *Jack you fucking ruined my good mood.*

"We manage," I said and tucked the check into the back pocket of my shorts. Today I was wearing my cutoffs, my bright pink cowboy boots, and a thin black tank top with a hot pink strappy bra underneath. I'd dressed this morning for my cowboy carpenter. My backyard voyeur. If he knew who I was, he didn't let on. But I got the sense he had no idea it was Bea King up there. Just like I couldn't guess who he was.

He was blond and he limped. He was pretty jacked, or at least his arm was. He was oddly polite and careful with that little throat-clearing system. And he turned me on like a blowtorch.

That was it.

There was a chance I'd walked by him a million times and just never noticed him. I could have served him, right here every day, but I just couldn't believe that. I was sure if I saw him outside of that yard again, I'd recognize him.

My body would. Like a magnet and true north.

"Hey," Jack said when I was halfway to the door. "Demolition started on the building next door."

"No kidding?" I laughed. "You know when knowing that would have been helpful?"

"Yesterday."

"Yeah. Any reason why it's happening at dawn?"

"Because my contractor has another job he has to get to."

"Contractor?" I said it so casually. Sooooooo casually. I almost believed myself that I didn't care so much about his name.

"Cody."

Cody? My entire body went to attention.

"His name is Cody?" Shit. I couldn't help myself.

"Yeah, good guy. Really keeps to himself so don't—"

"Don't what?"

"Harass him."

I stuck my tongue out at him.

His name was Cody. My cowboy voyeur's name was Cody.

I put that name away like a secret.

"Hey," I said. "Could you...just don't tell him my name?"

"Why would I tell him your name?"

"I don't know. You just let his name slip pretty easy."

"I didn't think it was a secret."

Oh my God, I am making this so weird.

"I just don't need someone with a grudge against my Daddy-"

"Cody does not give a crap about Hank King. He barely lived here. I'm not sure he even knows The Kings."

I shot him a skeptical look. Everyone knows The Kings.

"So, what happens after demolition?" I asked, changing the subject because I could feel my face getting hot.

"Construction. For about two weeks."

"Are you closing down The Bar? Because staff needs to know—"

"Hold on there, management," he said, a twinkle in his eye. "I'll let the staff know when I know. I'm hoping not to have to close down. But I have to see what my architect says."

"Right," I said, grabbing my purse from behind the bar. "That sounds like a problem I'm glad I don't have to worry about. Since I'm just an employee. See you tomorrow."

The front door of Jack's swung open, letting some of the bright Texas afternoon into the murky bar. And three big guys came in with the blinding sunlight and the three-hundred-percent humidity.

Danny Kincaid's red hair and freckles stood out against

his pale skin and I stepped to the left to give him a wide berth. "Hey there, Bea," he said, stopping when he saw me. "You leaving?"

"Shift's over," I said, giving him no smile. Because the guy could manufacture encouragement out of thin air. Give him a smile and the asshole got handsy. I'd had more than enough of Danny Kincaid in my time behind this bar.

"Come and have a drink with us, honey," he said, and my stomach curdled at the endearment. The man could take a sweet word like *honey* and make it rotten.

"Gotta go," I said.

His friends had walked on and he lurched sideways into my path. "You fucking King girls," he murmured. "Always acting like your shit don't stink."

"What can I say, Danny?" I curled my hand into a fist. The thing with assholes like Danny is that they expected a smack or a knee to the balls. What they didn't know was that I went right for the throat. One solid punch just under his flabby second chin and he'd be on the floor. Honest to god, I hoped he'd give me a reason. "We were actually blessed with shit that doesn't stink. A gift from our mother. I could bring you some, tomorrow morning—"

"Your money don't make you special," he hissed.

"You're right. But my tits do. Get out of my way, Danny."

Yeah, yeah, my mistake for bringing attention to my tits, but they were spectacular. His eyes took a long slow walk over my chest and I cocked back my fist ready to put him on the floor. But Jack was there and I gave Jack a whole lot of credit—he ran this place right.

"Danny," he said. "We've talked about this."

"I didn't touch her," he said, putting his hands up. "We were just talking."

"Don't try that bullshit with me," Jack said. "Go have beers some other place."

I blinked but I wasn't surprised. Not really. Jack was a good guy.

"Fuck that," Danny sneered. He tried to rally the guys he'd come in with, but Kimmy was already bringing them fresh, cold pint glasses of beer and the boys weren't moving.

"Your friends are choosing their beer over you," I laughed. "That must feel great."

Jack glared at me and Danny turned bright red.

"Come on," Jack said. "Head on out before things escalate."

Danny finally left and Jack spun to face me. "You always need to have the last word like that?" he asked.

"It's a genetic condition," I said.

He shook his head at me, not charmed in the slightest. "One of these days that mouth of yours is gonna get you in trouble."

It already had. More than once. My other great skill— not learning lessons the first time around. Or the second. Or the tenth.

"Come on," he said. "I'll walk you out. Just in case Danny is sticking around."

I protested that I was just going upstairs where I had a mastiff as a roommate, but Jack insisted.

"Hey," he said, once I got my door open. "I get why you don't want some stranger to know you live up here alone. And that you're a King. The wrong kind of guy would see that as an invitation to be an ass. Cody is not that guy, but I'll respect your privacy."

"Thanks Jack. You really are one of the good guys."

He tipped an imaginary hat and walked away. Not once had that guy hit on me. Or on any waitress. Or patron, now that I thought about it. In fact, I had never heard a single rumor in town about him with anyone.

Strange.

The dogs heard me coming and I climbed the stairs to my apartment listening to their claws on the hardwood as they scrambled to greet me at the door. Once I unlocked that door, it was total Armageddon. Thelma and Louise battled to get petted first. Thelma was bigger but Louise was louder, and in the end I just sat down in my doorway and scratched and rubbed both of them.

"I missed you, too!" I cried, accepting their licks and body wags. When they calmed down slightly I got to my feet to see what the damage was this time. One eviscerated pillow. A knocked-over ficus. And Louise had peed on the dining room table, because that girl knew how to make a point.

Neither one of them, sitting side by side, tails swishing across the floor, even managed to look guilty. "What am I going to do with you?" I asked them.

Louise woofed. Thelma whined.

"You want to go see Oscar?"

They jumped up with delight. My heart sank to my feet.

They loved Oscar. And Oscar lived on The King's Land.

Which meant I was going home.

I COULDN'T COUNT the number of times I'd taken Old Flagg Road out as far as it could go and then turned left until it hit The King's Land. When Veronica, Sabrina, and I went to high school in Dusty Creek, Veronica drove and Sabrina and I battled it out for the passenger seat.

God, that seemed like a million years ago. And yesterday, all at the same time.

The top was down on the Jeep and the dust and wind and sunlight whipped my hair into a rat's nest but the dogs sat in the back and loved it. They closed their eyes, let their tongues out to taste the air, and just basically lived their best dog lives.

I needed to get a bigger place.

But what if I bought a house and decided in a few weeks I wanted to go to college? What if I got a new apartment and in a few weeks decided I hated Dusty Creek? What if I made a decision and it was the wrong one?

"I'm sorry," I said to my dogs. "Honestly, guys. It's just for a few more weeks."

But I'd been saying that for the better part of a year. They didn't even respond, like they knew I was lying.

I turned left off Old Flagg Road toward where the gates to The King's Land crossed the gravel a few miles later. The gates were open, and as I pulled around the circular driveway to the front of the mansion I saw a sporty red Porsche SUV and smiled.

Ronnie was here. And wherever Ronnie was, Clayton followed.

I loved my sister. And I'd even grown to like my new brother-in-law, largely because his devotion to my sister was profound.

But the questions about what I was going to do with my life were doubled when Clayton was around. Clayton and Ronnie really liked answers and my current lack of them made them very antsy.

It would have been entertaining if I wasn't on the other side of it.

The car was barely in park before Thelma had leaped

out the back. Louise, the chicken, barked to be picked up and set down on the dirt. Which I did. Because Louise was my queen.

The house was a beauty, despite my father and my step-mother's efforts to ruin it. Brick and columns and two wings swinging off to the sides. It was a Texas-size mansion. Inside it was hideous, but the outside looked like something on a TV show.

My body shuddered just looking at it. The worst days of my life were spent in this house. My soul had been dimin-ished and my spirit ridiculed. I was made to feel a kind of shame that I've never been able to shake off.

Bea the Fuck-Up was born in this house. And I hated it.

The front door opened and Ronnie stepped out onto the wide porch. Despite hating the house and dreading the questions she would ask me, I was so happy to see her. And by her screams, she was pretty happy to see me.

She looked amazing. Being loved by Clayton had trans-formed my sister. Her hair was the same, and she was wearing a dress we'd bought together in Austin a million years ago. But she just...glowed.

"What are you doing here?" she cried, running down the steps to sweep me up in her arms.

"Me? What are you doing here?"

I hugged her as hard as she hugged me. And I buried my head in her neck and smelled her—lavender and Pantene shampoo and home.

My sister and I had lived together for five years in Austin and so the dogs claimed her as their human, too, and wiggled their way between us, barking until Ronnie acknowledged them.

"Seriously," I said as Ronnie scrubbed bellies and

accepted face licks from the dogs. "What are you doing here?"

"We need to do something about this house," she said. "I don't want it. Sabrina doesn't want it. Dylan doesn't—"

"Sell it," I said.

"Well," Ronnie said. "There's more to it than that. We might not want the house, but do we want to sell the land? The stables?"

"Keep the stables, sell the land."

"You know it's not that easy."

I thought it was exactly that easy. Ronnie tended to make things more complicated the more she thought about them.

Sometimes you just had to go with your gut, you know?

"Why not?" I asked. "Aren't Oscar and Maria ready to retire? They've got grandkids in Galveston and they just put a down payment on an RV. You don't need to worry about them. I vote sell everything. Sell it all. Every stick."

"Noted," she said.

The front door opened again and there was Clayton. Handsome, super-rich, totally devoted to my sister Clayton. For all those things you'd think I would like him. Love him, even. But before he made my sister the happiest woman in the world, he destroyed her.

The only one not totally over it was me. I'd had front-row seats to my sister's devastation and carried a grudge. As her sister, it was my job.

"Bea," he said, smiling a little as he stepped up beside Ronnie. "I didn't know you were meeting us."

"I'm not," I said. "I'm here to give the dogs a chance to run." I looked down at the dogs who were flopped at my feet, tongues out in the June heat.

"You have three million dollars in a bank account,"

Clayton said. "Why don't you get a house with a yard so they can run there?"

My sister reached over and stroked his arm, some kind of married couple communication for *it's not your business.* Or something. I didn't speak the language. But Clayton nodded tersely and the subject was dropped.

Clayton's phone rang and he stepped away to answer it.

"Do you need some help?" Ronnie asked me.

"With what?"

"With... " She shrugged. "Anything."

Anything was code for my life.

"Everything is fine, Ronnie." I didn't even try not to sound peeved. She wasn't being pushy, she was just doing what...we do.

"You know what I mean. Figuring out what to do next. Going back to college."

When Clayton destroyed her life years ago, I'd been there and I picked up the pieces of my sister. And she's been paying me back ever since by fixing my problems. Keeping me out of trouble. Making decisions so I wouldn't have to.

And I have let her, for an embarrassingly long period of time.

Not healthy.

"I can do this, Ronnie," I said. "I can figure out what's next on my own."

"I know," she said, quick with an empathic nod like it had never occurred to her to doubt me, which we both knew was far from the truth. I was Bea King—doubting me was the second biggest religion in Dusty Creek right behind high school football. "It's just that...you haven't. And I want you to know that I'm here. If you need me."

"You kidding?" I asked and tucked my arm in hers. We stepped off the paved path to the house, into the scrubby grass that used to be lush and green but had been left to go brown in the heat. "The prevailing truth in my life is that you are here for me."

She smiled and pressed her head into mine. The dogs, once their humans were on the move, got up and trotted behind us. Occasionally Louise barked at some groundhog or butterfly and Thelma would go darting off into the underbrush to hunt some squirrel that she didn't have a chance in hell of catching.

"Tell me what's going on with you," I said, changing the subject away from me.

"We're going to New York tomorrow. I have a few meetings for the foundation. We're going to be back at the end of the month for dinner at Sabrina and Garrett's. You should come!"

"She already invited me."

"Great, then I'll see you there."

"I'm busy."

"Bea," she sighed.

"I am. I am way too busy doing anything but watching my two sisters have a competition about who is more in love."

"It's not a competition," Ronnie said with a smile. "I win, hands down. I know you're on some kind of self-inflicted abstinence, but you should consider it."

"Love?"

"Yeah. It's...really nice."

I couldn't tell my sister, who looked like she was made of light and kittens, that all I knew about love—really knew, like down in the soles of my feet—was that it was a seesaw. The higher it lifted you, the deeper it would drop you.

And she should know that, considering what Clayton had done to her.

It was for fools. And I was no longer a fool.

I hugged my sister close and thought about the things I could say.

You're crazy to love this much.

Loving someone is no guarantee they'll love you back.

But I squeezed my sister and kept my mouth shut.

3

C ODY

THURSDAY MORNING I was out there again. My leg was killing me but I was standing in the back of that yard, rubbing my knee, watching that deck up in the leaves. Waiting.

What the fuck am I doing?

What was *she* doing?

If I were a smarter guy maybe I'd have the words for this.

Was there a word for this?

Voyeurism wasn't it.

Because I made sure I couldn't see her. Not all of her. That big old oak made getting a good look at her next to impossible. I could move, find a spot in the yard where the giant tree didn't make seeing her difficult, but this suited me just fine.

Yesterday, right here, under these branches, I hadn't been able to see her face or see much of her at all. When she sat I'd taken one step back and to the left so I could see her hands as she put them between her legs. And I could hear her. And I could imagine...

The way I was living these days and what I'd been through, she seemed like a fucking miracle.

There was a chance she wouldn't show this morning. And I couldn't blame her. She was taking on a lot of risk without knowing if I was some kind of maniac who meant her harm.

For the eight hundredth time I glanced around the yard, making sure there was no one else back here. Not on the construction site, not on The Bar's back deck. No one but me.

What a noble pervert I was.

Anticipation was like a shot of whiskey on an empty stomach.

The deck door was pulled open, the dogs came charging out for breakfast and she followed, wearing another oversize T-shirt.

Oh. Thank God. The relief was almost embarrassing.

She turned and I could see her shirt said Fuck the Patriarchy in big white letters.

Boldness seemed to be her calling card and all the parts of me I'd locked up clamored to get loose. Clamored for her.

When she set the food down, the dogs went bonkers for it and I cleared my throat. A subtle little signal that I was there. Watching. She laughed in her throat as she stood up—part laugh, part moan. One hundred percent kerosene.

She ran her hand up her thigh as she stood, so I could see the scrap of red lace under the shirt.

This woman was going to kill me.

Once the dogs were done eating she shifted the chair so

it faced me directly and I stepped to the side, a little farther into the trees so I could see her without totally seeing her.

I was pretty fucked up these days and had a hard time really being clear on what was important, but we'd avoided seeing each other's faces, and that seemed like something I had to protect at all costs. From this spot, the oak tree and the banister obscured her face but between the leaves and the wrought-iron spindles of the railing I could see that sweet spot between her legs.

She propped one bare foot on the seat and stretched her other leg out wide. The navy blue shirt dipped down between her legs.

I knew better than to wish for anything. It was a miracle she was doing this at all and I had no business wanting more. But for a second, the force with which I wanted that tail of blue shirt to be lifted up and out of the way almost brought me to my knees.

Then she slipped her fingers beneath the lace of the underwear and moaned low in her chest. And I wondered if it was because it felt so good or because she knew I could hear it. I wanted it to be both. I wanted the show and her authenticity.

I wanted her to like doing this for me. For her to be as turned on as I was.

My erection was its own beast, and I throbbed and ached against the zipper of my jeans but I didn't dare touch myself. I didn't dare adjust my cock or I'd risk coming like a teenage boy. So I clenched my hands into fists until they hurt.

She lifted the shirt so I could see the top lace of her red underwear and her hand reaching down to pull the lace to the side of her pussy. I imagined how pink she would be. How wet.

I groaned, low in my throat. I just wanted to say something to her. I wanted to be as much a part of this as I could.

She spread her legs out wider and rocked forward in her
chair. Presenting herself to me and I fucking loved that. I
went from hard to concrete.

"I can see you." Her voice was barely a whisper, but I
jumped like she'd electrocuted me.

Even the blood in my veins went still. I wasn't sure my
lungs could work. And for a second the impulse to turn and
walk away was so strong I had to close my eyes just to keep
myself there.

"Not all of you," she said, and I exhaled long and slow.
"That fist you're making," she said. "I can see that."

Again, I looked around, making sure we were alone. But
there was no one back here. It was the ravine on one side,
Jack's empty deck on the other, and a brick wall on the other
side of that.

It was just us.

She flipped the blue shirt back down so the view was
obscured.

"You want to see more?" she asked.

"Yes."

My voice sounded like it was being pulled out of
my boots.

"Then show me something."

I wanted to climb up on that second-floor deck and bury
myself between her legs. I wanted to make her come for
days until the fire under my skin was gone. I wanted to fuck
her until I could stand myself again.

But that wasn't what she was offering, and even if it had
been I'd never take it. There were rules here. And I knew
what she wanted.

"The risk is what makes it hot, cowboy," she said, all

teasing and coy.

I took my time undoing my belt, unzipping my fly, all with the arm she said she could see. As far as stripteases went, it was pretty lame, but it seemed like the bark of that big old tree was starting to smoke.

My cock, once I had my zipper down and my boxer briefs out of the way, was leaking come all over the place. This, I thought, looking down at myself, was going to be a very short show. But I took my cock in my hand, hissing at the contact, my own touch made revolutionary just because she was watching. I lifted my fist and licked the slick of come off my fingers.

"Oh, my god," she gasped. "That…"

She liked that. So I did it again. And she rewarded me by lifting her shirt out the way. She rubbed her clit and then she used her other hand to fuck herself and…fuck.

I started working myself over good.

And there was twenty feet of angles and oak tree between us, keeping us separate. Keeping us secret. But that moment, even not seeing her face or most of her body, was the most intimate thing I'd ever experienced.

I looked away, broke the moment because my fight-or-flight instinct kicked in hard. But for my body it was too late. One hard stroke and I was done, coming into my hand, biting my lip so I didn't make any sound.

Up there she was coming, too. I could hear the soft gasps and pants she made when she fucked herself to orgasm. She sprawled back in her seat, and I imagined I could smell her on the breeze. The salty sweetness of her. I imagined her body, replete in that chair. The nape of her neck would be sweaty. Her pussy when I touched it would be hot. Swollen.

"Hey," she whispered. "You…okay?"

Without another word I turned and walked away.

4

B EA

LOUISE WOKE me up from a delicious dream about Ryan Gosling cooking me a steak dinner by lying with her belly across my mouth and suffocating me.

"Okay," I muttered, pushing Louise away from my face. "I'm up. I'm up. And you need a bath."

Once up, I was up. Like, for-real up. I shoved my feet into some shoes and took the dogs out to the ravine.

I kept one eye out for Sabrina but she didn't show up. She often didn't on Fridays. And I was glad. I was.

But I kind of wanted to tell her about this thing. This morning thing I was doing with the strange man in the backyard. She'd get scandalized and her eyes would go wide and she'd be a little judgy, but she'd also want to know more.

My cowboy voyeur was a hot secret, but what fun was a

secret if you couldn't talk about it with someone? And Sabrina was all I had. Except, it would seem, I didn't even have her.

The air smelled like butter and sugar, and I could see the lights on in Sweet Things, but she stayed on her side of the street.

And I stayed on mine.

Ronnie would be so disappointed in us.

My hands trailed across the old wood paneling of the stairwell and came away covered in dust. Everything was filthy because of the work Cody was doing.

Cody.

His name was Cody. Cody watched me jack myself off. Cody watched when I bent over showing him all my secrets. Cody who licked the come off his hand and made that little coughing sound to tell me he was there. Cody who warned me I wasn't alone when I felt so fucking alone all the damn time.

Cody. I'd spent the last two nights staring up at my ceiling, thinking his name until I whispered it out loud. And then immediately felt foolish. Louise had poked her head up over the edge of my mattress and barked at me as if in agreement.

He was already out there; I'd heard him after the dogs woke me up.

What to do? I thought. What to do for him? For us? Because there was no pretending I wasn't into this just as much as he was, if not more.

While the dogs were peeing and sniffing around, the first drops of rain fell from the heavy sky. And the earth opened up, letting loose the scent of summer. A dusty, earthy, green and thirsty smell. It was delicious.

The dogs charged up from the ravine and into the open

side door behind me. Upstairs I changed out of my boots and sleep shorts and into a plain white T-shirt that hung just past my butt. Rain pattered against the window, big, fat drops. Without any escalation.

Underwear? No underwear?

I decided none, poured a bunch of kibble into the two dog bowls, and opened the screen door with my shoulder and elbow. The dogs poured out, jumping up and down on my small deck waiting for their food.

Cody.

When I was a kid I'd gone to one homecoming dance. I'd been a freshman and not yet a total cynic, my date had been a junior, and I'd been giddy with anticipation. I'd had to put my fingers to my lips to keep inside these wild giggles that kept wanting to erupt. The night had ended terribly, but that feeling had been worth it.

And standing on my deck, I felt the exact same way.

New. Excited. And full of possibility.

I pressed my fingers to my lips, keeping in the wild giggles.

He was out there. I could see a different slice of him this time. His chin and chest. His mouth. Jesus...his mouth. It was set in a firm line but it was a good mouth. I wanted that mouth on mine. On my body.

No. Nope. Rein it in.

The rain didn't bother the dogs any and it hit my shirt, my shoulders, and my hair in big fat drops.

Facing away from Cody, I bent to put the bowls on the ground and in the backyard, instead of his usual throat clearing, I heard him groan.

"Sweet Jesus."

I smiled to myself and stood back up while the dogs

cleared out their bowls with record speed and then beelined back inside.

With my face tilted up to the rain I turned and faced the backyard, and I didn't have to look to see what was happening with my shirt. The transparent spots revealed the pink of my flesh beneath the thin white material. I looked glazed in sugar. Sweet and pink. Delicious.

My skin was soon slick, my short hair damp. I looked down at the spot where he usually sat and I saw his boots and the worn denim he wore, even in this heat.

My shirt was soaked through; from his angle I imagined he could see my nipples, pulled into hard brown beads from the rain, the dark nest of curls between my legs. I turned again, imagining the shirt clinging to the round curves of my ass, and my hearing was so attuned to him, so thirsty to hear every single sound from his mouth, I could hear him moan low in his throat.

And the sound rippled up my spine, over all my skin. And I wanted him to touch me. My hands were suddenly not enough.

Stunned by the realization, I froze. I should have seen this coming. This was the most Bea thing I could possibly do—take a good thing and ruin it by wanting more.

But suddenly, with the sound of that groan, I wanted his hand on my body. The heavy calluses. The heat and heft of a man at my back. I arched my spine, imagining him behind me. I touched the flat, muscular planes of my stomach and imagined my hands were his. I gathered my shirt in rough fists and wished it was his rough touch on my body.

I imagined him bending me over the railing, pushing my bare feet out wide his with boots. I imagined the scrape of his jeans against the bare skin of my legs. The feel of his erection behind that zipper pressed into the cleft of my ass.

Fuck.

This...fuck.

I opened my eyes and stopped. Just...stopped. My hands dropped my shirt and I just stood there on the porch, letting the rain fall down on me. My shirt was soaked now and I had to figure he was standing down there getting pretty soaked, too.

"You okay?" His voice floated up from behind those oak leaves. It was still shocking to hear him talk.

Of course. Being okay, being better than okay, was kind of a way of life for me. A trick of the rain and a tiny wiggling worm of loneliness weren't going to change that.

"Yeah," I said. My voice a little louder so he could hear me above the sound of the rain.

"You're getting soaked," he said, like he cared.

Oh, don't do that, buddy. Whatever you do, don't do that.

I sat in the chair I had positioned exactly for this reason. And the rain made the leaves heavy so I could see a little more of him than I usually could. His hat was tipped down over his face. So I couldn't see his eyes, but I could feel them. I could feel him watching me. His jeans were damp from the rain, molded to hard thighs.

He was thin but strong, and standing there getting wet, his body was divine.

He slipped one hand up the inside of his thigh to cup himself through that faded thin denim. And I went wet. Just totally wet. I couldn't get my legs parted wide enough fast enough and flipped my wet shirt up.

"Fuck," he breathed, and I was so glad I'd decided no underwear. And I slipped my fingers between the fat wet lips of my pussy and found my clit, so hard. So ready.

One touch and I was panting. My muscles bracing themselves.

"You," I said, and I hadn't even finished the word before he had the button of his jeans popped and the zipper undone.

I could see his cock. Most of it, anyway. And I felt suddenly empty in all the places where that cock would go.

It was partly the rain, and partly my anger with myself for imagining him when I wasn't supposed to be doing that, and almost entirely the sight of him with his heavy cock in his hand, but my touch was almost angry. I used myself hard because I liked it that way, too. And if his groans were anything to go by, so did he.

My fingers blazed over my clit, a hard, fast rub that made me bend my head and close my eyes and wish, so hard in that unguarded moment right before the orgasm swept me up, that it was his touch making me crazy. That they were his fingers I was coming on.

"Fuck!" I groaned through my teeth, and I clamped my legs together over my hand and rode my wrist until I was done. Used up. My legs fell open again and I lifted my hand, wincing at the inadvertent touch on my sensitive skin.

Out in the backyard, my carpenter cowboy was still going, his hand a blur over the shaft of his cock, and for a second, watching his hand, I could imagine it was my hand. I wished it was my hand. And I closed my eyes and made a fist out of my palms and fingers, and if I concentrated there it was. The hard girth of him. The soft, silky heat. From there it was nothing to imagine his voice in my ear. Maybe his hand on the back of my head, urging me down until my lips touched the crown of his dick.

"Take it," he might whisper. "Suck me."

And I'd be on my knees in a second. A heartbeat.

Oh, fuck, my fingers eased back between my legs and my orgasm, when I came again, was harder and longer. A deep wave from inside my body, the slow excruciating push up and the ecstatic wild pulse down.

And I never closed my eyes. I kept them open, watching him finish. He curled over himself as if hiding or protecting this vulnerable minute. Both his hands were between his legs and I didn't know what he was doing but I imagined plenty.

And wanted even more.

Then it was over. Both of us sat there, panting. Sweating in the rain. I sucked the water off my lips and tasted my own sweat.

"You okay?" he asked.

I nodded, my voice shot. He couldn't see me. Or see me nod.

"Yeah," I croaked.

The rain was speeding up. And it was growing cool. Goose bumps rose up over my skin and I pushed my shirt down over my legs.

He zipped up his pants and braced his hands on his knees like he needed to gather himself for a second. And how badly I wanted him to come upstairs was terrifying. How much I wanted him, even after those two orgasms, was problematic.

"Hey," I called out. "You could come up."

There. The words were out. He didn't move and I thought maybe he hadn't heard me over the rain. But then he shook his head, a hard shake. No.

And as if that was the push he needed, he walked away. Out of sight.

5

C ODY

ON FRIDAY NIGHT the knock on the door could only be Jack, and you could always count on Jack to have beer. Even before he owned a bar, he would show up with a six-pack. Even in that juvie camp we got sent to, where we met as kids, the one that was more prison than the prisons I'd been in, Jack had managed to smuggle in a six-pack of Bud.

The guy was goddamn magic.

I made my way to the door as quick as I could, but the knee was stiff in the evening and the pain radiated all the way up my side so my walk was more of a hop, but I threw open the door.

"Took you long enough," Jack said, standing under the porch light with the moths buzzing around his head.

"Fuck you."

Jack smiled at me, I smiled back and stepped aside so he

could come in with his beer and the to-go box he had with him. Wings from the smell of it.

Fuck. I was starving. The smell of those wings made my mouth water.

Jack set the to-go container on the table along with the six-pack of Shiner. We both looked down at it.

"This is a shitty date," Jack said, and I laughed.

"Especially since neither one of us is getting lucky."

Jack looked at me sideways, wiggling his eyebrows.

"I'm not your type and we both know it," I said with another laugh.

"It's true." He sighed heavily.

"Have you heard from her?" I asked, watching him out of the corner of my eyes. This wasn't something we talked about much. Used to be he never shut up about Natalie. But it had been years since he'd mentioned her name.

"Cody?" Jack sighed. "Can we...not."

"Yeah. Sure." Gladly, I left the subject of Natalie alone.

I led him into my grandmother's old dining room that had all her fancy plates on the walls and the smell of her pies somehow still in the air. The tiny one-story house was practically made of Gran's favorite colors—green and yellow. If the walls weren't green, they were yellow, and the few that were neither were covered in pictures of daises and daffodils and green meadows. Even those old plates on the wall were green and yellow.

It was manically cheerful. Kind of like Gran.

She'd died about six months ago, just before the accident.

A few people in my life had called it lucky, my gran dying right about the time I needed a place to live.

Those people were no longer in my life.

"You just never really get used to it, do you?" Jack asked, looking around the dining room.

"Not really," I said, easing into a chair at the long pine dining table. I ate about a million cherry pies at this table. Roast beef after Sunday church. Grilled cheese for Saturday-night dinners. Gran poured me my first whiskey at this table one Sunday night when I was fifteen and got released from that camp. The whiskey was supposed to help the news that my mom wouldn't be coming to pick me up go down a little easier.

I'd shot back the whiskey and told Gran I was happy to stay with her.

Six months ago—crazy with grief—I'd wanted to bury the table with her. Like a demented cowboy berserker I'd demanded Howie at the funeral home figure out how to do it.

I'd been so fucking out of my head.

Jack had talked me down arranged to have the corner next to her old spot at the head of the table shaved off and set in her casket.

"So," he said, cracking open a beer and handing it to me. I opened the wings and we dug in. "How is progress?"

"All the walls are down. The electrical is a wreck—"

"Can you fix it?"

I put down the chicken wing. "I really don't know where you're getting the idea that I'm trained—"

"Can you fix it?"

"Yeah, but—"

"Great." Jack took a bite of a wing and waggled his eyebrows at me like he'd tricked me into something. I knew the basics of construction from my early years working odd jobs on the regional rodeo circuit, and on the threadbare value of my name I'd gotten a quarter-time job sanding drywall for literally pennies on a new build south of town.

Jack gestured with his bottle toward my knee. "How is rehab?"

"You are some kind of old lady with this shit—"

"Are you not doing the exercises?"

"Yeah. I'm doing the fucking exercises."

"And?"

"And I'm ready for the ballet." I held out my arms. "Wanna see?"

"Cody," Jack sighed. And if it was anyone else sighing at me like that I'd put my fist in their face, but from my oldest friend and one of my current bosses and the guy buying me dinner—I'd let a few sighs go.

"I'm walking. I'm doing demo. Hurts like hell at night, but I can handle it." I shrugged. "It's more than they thought I'd do five months ago."

"The meds?"

I shook my head. I'd gotten off that poison as fast as I could.

"And Bonnie?"

I glanced away at the mention of her name.

"Also walking." I nodded carefully, trying to be cool in the face of all the complicated shit just saying that made me feel. The cost of rehab for the two of us was eating up every penny my jobs were paying me. But it was worth it.

Jack touched the edge of his bottle to the edge of mine. "To both of you walking," he said. He took a sip and I set down my beer. I wanted to ask him about the girl. The woman on the deck.

My Morning Girl. Stupid name, I know.

No one ever accused me of being the smartest guy and I

didn't have a single word for what we were doing. She left me speechless.

She left me so damn hungry.

There'd been a period of time in the rodeo, after I'd nearly blown it all first time, when I'd lived impossibly clean. No beer. No booze. Healthy food. I ran most mornings. Avoided the women whose arms I usually rushed right into. And Charlie...fuck, Charlie. I hadn't thought of him in so long...had told me denying myself everything only meant that sooner or later I'd break in a big way.

Give yourself something, he'd said. *A little something sweet.*

At first I hadn't listened. I'd scoffed at him. And I'd lived in this slim little slice of my life. So sanctimonious. Healthy as fuck, but barely holding on.

And what do you know, Charlie was right. After a big loss, I'd swan dived off every single wagon I'd been living on in a week-long bender of beer and drugs and burgers. And then spent another week regretting it. Hungover and sick to my stomach. Later, there were prescription antibiotics for the STD I'd gotten.

It had been a good lesson that I'd learned by heart.

And my Morning Girl was supposed to be that something sweet to get me through these bleak weeks while I figured out who I was without rodeo. A gift I gave myself so I didn't go screaming into the abyss.

But this morning it had looked like she'd been dipped in sugar and water, and I'd had to physically stop myself from going up there. From climbing the tree and jumping her wrought-iron railing and licking the water from her pink skin. Nudging that T-shirt up above that round ass...

What. The. Hell.

No talking. No names. No seeing each other's faces.

And those rules were there for a good goddamn reason.

And I nearly broke every last one of them. I nearly broke my own hands keeping myself in that backyard.

Away from her. I didn't need to ask. I didn't really want to know. Because there was seriously nothing I could do about it. I couldn't take her out to dinner. Or for a drink. I didn't even have condoms right now and they weren't in the budget for next week, either.

But somehow—I couldn't stop myself. "Hey, Jack, the woman—"

"I need you to quit that other job of yours," he said at the same time.

"The Bruns build?"

"Yeah. You've gotta quit." He leaned back in his chair, crossing his hands over the Dr. Who shirt he wore.

I laughed. This was why I liked Jack. Had always liked Jack. When we met I was so mad I was taking swings at everything that moved. And he'd made me laugh.

"And do what?" I asked, picking my beer back up.

"Work for me. To get the bar built. Be my general contractor. Full time."

"Are you high?"

"Not for too many years," he said sadly.

I stretched my leg out straight and looked at my big toe sticking out of my good pair of socks. I was wearing my good jeans, too. And one of my five T-shirts. These clothes, a warm coat, and my boots were all I had.

"Can you pay me?" I asked, wiggling my toe at myself.

"With love?"

"Jack?"

"Of course I can fucking pay you. Pay you better than that crap job you're working out there. Give you better experience. Build your resume. Introduce you to my architect and maybe you've got a chance at a full-time job as a part of her crew."

"That's nice of you, Jack. Real nice. But what do you get out of it?"

"What are you talking about?" he cried.

"Oh my God, you need me to spell it out for you?" I asked.

He took a drink and nodded at me. "Spell it out, friend."

"I'm an injured rodeo cowboy with limited construction experience."

"You know, for such a hotshot, you're real good at selling yourself short, Cody. I trust you and I just need someone to keep it all together. I just need..."

Don't say a friend. Don't. Please. God. I might fucking cry.

"Someone I can trust," he finished and I relaxed into my chair. Trust I could handle. "Two weeks Cody. Help me out for two weeks."

This feeling...what was happening in my chest? In my brain? I hadn't felt it in months.

Pride. In myself. Purpose. A thing to wake up for.

God. Thank you, Jack.

"Cody?" He tilted his head at me. "Tell me you'll stick around."

"I'll need a raise."

He laughed. He laughed in that old Jack way and I lifted the beer to cover my smile. "Thanks, buddy. I knew I could count on you."

Yeah. In this wide world the two of us could count on each other.

"You know," Jack said, looking around. "It's not that I don't like hanging out in your grandmother's house as, like, an immersive 1970s experience—"

"Hey, now!" I said, feigning outrage. It was a bit of a time warp in this place between the shag carpet and the macramé, but I hadn't had the money or the inclination to change anything.

"You know I have a bar. With beer. And wings. And people. Actual people…girl people, too."

"I don't like bars," I said, digging into another wing.

"You used to love them."

Oh, I loved bars. The taste of whiskey in the back of my throat. A cold beer in my hand. The feel of a pretty stranger pressed up against my chest. The smell of sweat and possible sex and the unrelenting ease of it all.

Fuck. I loved bars.

It was a wonder I hadn't stepped back into one.

And maybe I could have bars back in moderation. Maybe I could have part of my life back. In moderation.

"Listen," Jack said, clapping me on the back. "Tomorrow. It's Saturday. You're not working. Come in for lunch."

"You've already done so much. No way am I letting you buy me lunch, too."

"Excellent. Come in and pay for your own lunch."

"Jack—"

"You can meet Bea. If she doesn't put a smile on your face, nothing will."

"Don't do that to the girl." I bristled up hard.

"What?"

"Try to fix her up with me."

"You should be so lucky to have her look your way, cowboy, but she's off men or some shit."

"Then why—?"

"She's the bartender," Jack said. "She'll pour you a beer. Tell you some bullshit story about something. Put a smile on your face. That's all. You remember how bars work, right?"

I could feel Jack looking at me, waiting for me to say no. To find an excuse.

He'd been good to me. The job. The beer. The friendship when everyone else had left. Or I'd pushed them away.

"Okay," I said, tossing bones into the nearly empty container. "But I hope you serve something better than these shitty wings."

He put his hand over heart like I'd deeply offended him.

"Hey," I said. "Can I ask you a question?"

"Depends."

"The girl who lives upstairs from the construction site?"

Jack pursed his lips. Shook his head. "I can't tell you."

"It's a secret?"

"No. She just likes her privacy. And asked me not to tell anyone."

"Really?" That seemed extreme, but then, maybe not. A woman who put on a show like that had to take some precautions.

"Is she giving you trouble out there?" Jack asked.

"Nope. I've barely even seen her."

6

Bea

HE WASN'T THERE on Saturday. The dogs did their business in the ravine. Sabrina didn't show and the backyard was quiet. Empty.

"Hello?" I called out. But only the wind answered. "You out here?"

Nothing.

And the disappointment was stupid. It was, in fact, so stupid that I pretended to be glad he wasn't there. Forced myself to be glad. Because he was a stranger and it was just a dumb lark and I had shit to do. Real shit.

Besides my clit was sore.

I cleaned my apartment top to bottom, emptying the vacuum canister of dog hair twice. And then I sat down with another cup of coffee and looked up fall courses at the community college about an hour away. I figured if I was going to go back to school I'd have to start small. No sense jumping into the deep end when I hadn't been to school in a whole bunch of years and had never been very good at it anyway.

The problem with the course book was that the only things that sounded interesting were the hospitality courses. Bar and Restaurant Management. Accounting for Small Businesses. And I'd already failed at that—why step up only to get knocked back down again?

At ten-thirty I kissed the dogs goodbye and headed downstairs to start the Saturday lunch shift, hoping something, anything, interesting might happen.

But it was unlikely.

CODY

I STOOD outside the front door of Jack's bar, staring at the dark wood door with the old Budweiser ad of that dog and wondered if I was in danger of breaking more rules.

Or was the fact that I was living the life of a hermit making me break those rules?

Fuck it. I was tired of second-guessing everything.

I put my hand to Spud's nose and pushed open the door.

There are a few places in my life that have smelled like home. A stable. Gran's. And a Texas dive bar. Fried food and beer. Decades-old cigarette smoke.

I filled my lungs with the smell and couldn't help the smile on my face.

My eyes adjusted to the relative darkness and I saw Jack and a woman at the corner of the bar, heads bent over paperwork. I stepped wide of them, leaving one stool between myself and them so I didn't interrupt them.

"Cody!" Jack greeted me like he couldn't believe I'd made it. Like I'd weathered some kind of storm to show up in his bar. "You're here."

"You invited me."

A tiny woman with short hair spun around from the corner of the bar where she'd been chatting with the waitress. She was a stunner, big eyes and bright red lips. Attitude that gave her a glow. Dark hair that was kind of curly and kind of spiky. She had a real pinup girl vibe going on. Sexy and tough all at once. A red handkerchief was tied in her hair that matched the ruby-red swipe of her lips. The black T-shirt with the collar torn out had silver glittery lettering across the front that I couldn't read.

God. I used to love bars. And sexy bartenders with bright red lips.

She watched me with her mouth open like I was a surprise, and for a moment I was all caught up in those eyes and lips. The pretty dip of skin beneath her collarbone that peeked through that torn collar.

And the sense that somehow we knew each other.

"Glad you're here," Jack said to me, pulling my attention from the pinup girl at the end of the bar. "Cody, this is Denise. She's my engineer for the project next door."

"Hi, Denise," I said and leaned over to shake the black woman's hand. Her hair and nails were cut short and her hand, when we shook, was covered in calluses. This was a woman who got her hands dirty. "Nice to meet you."

"Likewise," she said. "I understand you've been doing the demo."

"He'll be sticking around as my eyes on the job," Jack said.

"I've been wondering when you were going to hire a general contractor."

"I'm not a general—"

Jack wouldn't even let me finish that sentence. "Cody's my guy."

"Well, the crew you'll be working with are good guys," she said. "I'd usually stay on as contractor but we're spread a little thin this season."

"I'm happy to help out," I said.

Jack winked at me.

"We're going to do a walk-through after this meeting," Denise said, like she was going to check my work. She was the kind of person that made me hope I hadn't missed anything.

"I thought you weren't starting yet." I said, trying to sound anything but upset about that.

Because once they started, that was it for my mornings. There'd be a crew of guys over there. I wished I'd had a chance to say goodbye to my Morning Girl. But maybe this was better. Clean break and all that. And probably just in the nick of time.

I wasn't going to be able to resist her if she invited me up again. That was just a fact.

"My crew can't get in for another week," she said.

"A week?" Jack cried.

"Jack," she said calmly. "We talked about this."

"Can I get you something to drink?" the bartender asked while Jack and Denise argued timelines.

The bartender's voice was husky and all kinds of Texas. Now that she was standing right in front of me I saw that her shirt said Cut a Bitch.

"Coke is good," I said.

"Get him a burger, too, would you, Bea?" Jack asked. Ah,

this was the bartender who would make me smile. I smiled at her. The cloth she was running through her hands fell onto the floor and she ducked down behind the bar to grab it.

"Sorry," Jack said when she popped back up. "Bea, this is Cody. He's been the guy doing the work next door. Cody, this is Bea she's—"

"His underappreciated bartender," she interrupted.

"I appreciate you plenty," Jack said.

"Nice to meet you, Bea," I held out my hand to shake hers but she turned to punch my order into the computer system behind her.

"Is the burger better than the wings?" I asked, quickly putting my hand back in my lap.

"No," Bea said over her shoulder.

"Bea!" Jack said, like she'd broken his heart.

"You want better food you need a better kitchen."

"We're building a better kitchen. You'd see that if you'd just look at the plans."

"To have a better kitchen you need a chef."

"I have one."

"You have an eighteen-year-old kid who has watched a couple Guy Fieri shows."

Jack was silent, pointing at the blueprints in front of him, begging his bartender—with puppy-dog eyes—to look at the plans.

Bea shook her head, turned, grabbed a glass, and used a scoop to fill it with ice.

She was wearing a pair of jeans that slipped down when she bent, revealing the top lace edge of her pink underwear.

I glanced away, feeling like a creeper for noticing.

"You're a smart man, Jack. I'm sure you figured out the

kitchen just fine," Bea said and set the Coke down in front of me.

"What's with your voice?" Jack asked her. "You're suddenly Ms. Texas?"

"Nothing. What's wrong with your face?"

Laughter barked out of my throat and everyone turned to stare at me. Too big a laugh for too small a dig but I wasn't used to being out with people. "What *is* wrong with your face?" I pulled the straw out of my Coke and took a drink.

"This isn't why I invited you for lunch," Jack grumbled. I caught Bea's eye and winked. She went so pink I felt like an ass for even that lame attempt at flirting.

"So, what are the full plans for next door?" I asked. "I've never seen them."

Jack scootched them over to me.

"A big deck back here," he said, pointing to that little patch of earth where I watched my Morning Girl.

"You gonna get rid of the tree?" I touched the little icon Denise had drawn for the tree I stood under while she rocked my world.

"No. The city will never let me clear that tree. It's practically a historical monument."

No shit, I thought. It needed a plaque commemorating my Morning Girl.

"But it will be trimmed back. A bigger kitchen here."

Bea super-casually leaned over to get a look. I leaned back so she could see better, glanced up, and caught her small smile.

She really was cute.

"Double fryer. Grill. Dishwasher," Jack said, pointing to blank spaces on the drawings. "A second bar," he said indicating another space.

Bea glanced behind herself. Turned herself around the

other way to face the mirror and bottles of liquor. "Right there?" she asked. Pointing at the wall behind the bar.

"Close enough," Denise said.

"Can you open the wall?" Bea asked.

"It's not load-bearing," Denise said.

"That would be cool," I said, because I could see what Bea was getting at.

"Right?" she asked, looking at me with her eyes wide.

"Right what?" Jack asked.

"Open the bar. Two sided. Keep the bottles in the back, but everyone can look through," she said.

"Or you could set up one of those circular shelves that spin," I said, remembering one of those in Alberta.

"So both bars share the bottles?" she asked me, as if Jack and Denise weren't there. "That's kinda fun."

"Well, I don't know if it's fun. But it stands out."

Jack blinked at Bea. And then blinked at me. I shrugged. Bea turned away and pulled two Bud Light drafts for the waitress waiting for them down at the service end of the bar.

"I told you you'd like her," Jack whispered.

"Stop," I whispered back.

"It's a great idea," Denise said and made a note in pencil on the drawings. "But you'll have to close down this bar for a while," she said in a tone of voice that implied she'd been saying this for a while.

"You're right," Jack said. "Two weeks?"

"I told you," Bea said.

Denise bent sideways and looked at me. "How long will it take you to take down that wall?"

I shrugged. "One day for demo. Another one to frame the space."

"Then two weeks should do it," Denise said and looked at me.

"Yep."

"Bea," Jack said, "Tuesday the bar is closed anyway. If we close down Monday can you come in and clean it up so Cody can tear it down?"

"Me?" she asked. "Monday's my day off."

"You. And I'll pay you."

"Double?"

"I'll pay you what I'd pay a manager."

She pursed her lips at him in a way I found really distracting.

"I'll help," I volunteered and tried not to regret it. This was a lot of socializing. She laughed like I didn't fool her, and I probably didn't. She looked like a woman who didn't fool easily.

I sat up straighter under her gaze. Felt a little bit like her eyes were searching me, picking through my pockets. Ruffling through my hair. Again, it was like I knew her.

And she knew me.

I coughed and turned my face away, the intimacy of her attention too much.

She sucked in a deep breath like she was committing to something more than emptying out a bar.

"All right," she said. "It's a date."

I held out my hand to shake on it but she'd already turned away.

7

B EA

AFTER CODY LEFT I braced my hands out wide on the bar and hung my head. My legs were literally weak. The effort of not blurting out, *It's me. The girl on the deck. Yesterday I got off twice to you getting off on me. Remember?*

The effort of not putting my hands into that thick blond hair. Not pressing my body against the hard, straight angles of his. Not touching that surprisingly beautiful, thick-lipped mouth.

God...that mouth of his.

His smile had about broken my heart.

I felt as if I'd run a mile as fast as I could. Sweat trickled down my back and I was sick with adrenaline.

I thought I knew that kind of pure chemistry. What I'd felt for Travis in the first few minutes after meeting him had felt big. Different. But this attraction with Cody made Travis seem lukewarm. Barely noticeable.

Trouble. He was one hundred percent pure trouble.

Cody.

His flirting was rusty but that cowboy charm was still there, behind some kind of damage. He wasn't used to being hesitant. That was obvious. He'd flashed that wink at me real fast, but then clearly wanted to take it back.

No. He used to be confident. He used to be sure.

Now he wasn't.

Part of not being Bea King meant not caring about what had happened to that cowboy. What put his charm behind ice. Not wanting to tease out that reluctant smile of his.

I put a hand against my chest and felt my beating heart. *Cody.*

My cowboy carpenter, my backyard voyeur, was so beautiful. More beautiful even than I'd dreamed. And when he'd held out his hand to shake mine—twice—I'd ignored it. Because I couldn't know how he felt. I couldn't know the warmth of his skin and the touch of his fingers.

I just couldn't.

"You okay?" Kimmy asked.

"No."

"Can I do anything?"

"No."

"Then I need two margaritas. Rocks."

I got out the rocks glasses and poured tequila, lime juice, Cointreau, and ice into my shaker and shook the fuck out of those margaritas.

There was a pit growing in my stomach. I should have told him who I was. Because surely Jack would let him know I was the girl living in that apartment. He almost had five minutes ago and would have if I hadn't interrupted. The truth was bound to come out. And it felt like a trick that I knew and he didn't.

And that accent I put on? Oh God, it was awful.

But I didn't know how to stand there in front of my boss and Denise and have that moment with him. That moment when he realized he'd seen my clit and I'd watched him come and now we had to make small talk.

I'd already been so vulnerable in front of him I couldn't imagine being more vulnerable.

What if he said something? Or laughed. Or...

He wouldn't. He wasn't that kind of guy. I knew that in my gut. But I wasn't going to beat myself up for wanting to control the moment.

Monday. I would tell him on Monday. In private. We'd have an awkward laugh and he'd ask me out and I'd have to tell him that I wasn't dating broken-down cowboys anymore. As a life rule.

Our mornings were over. Or would be the second we both knew.

"Who was that guy with Jack? The blond?" Kimmy asked.

"Guy working next door."

"Really?" Kimmy leaned against the bar, her hand on her hip, her high ponytail falling over her shoulder just right. "I wonder if he's seeing anyone."

Me, I wanted to say. Every morning. All day Monday.

Me. Me. Me.

Oh, God. I was in so much trouble.

CODY

.   .   .

MONDAY MORNING my Morning Girl was late. She hadn't even let the dogs out yet. The sun was bright and thick, and the humidity was intense. Sweat ran down my back and down the backs of my legs.

Even the oak tree seemed a little limp in the heat.

I wiped my face off with the hem of my shirt and left it soaked. I glanced at my watch, thinking I was wrong, but nope. It was now ten after seven and I could sense the town on the other side of the building waking up.

The air smelled like fresh coffee and not just baking from the bakery across the street, which meant the doors were open.

This wasn't a big deal. It wasn't. She just wasn't...there.

Was she sick? Was she okay?

Did something happen to the dogs?

I took a step toward the building, planning, without really thinking, to walk around and knock on her door. I stopped myself. If she walked out onto her porch, she walked out on the porch. And if she didn't...well, it wasn't my business, was it?

Except for the fact that I'd spent the weekend thinking about her.

I grocery shopped, and with the money left over from paying for Bonnie I was able to buy some milk and ten packages of ramen.

I did the crappy PT exercises, sweating through my shirt just bending my knee back and forth, sliding my foot across the floor. I did those exercises until I shook.

And I thought about her.

So. Much.

The sun was shining. There was a breeze moving through the leaves of the big oak tree.

It was 7:15 and then 7:30, and then I realized I'd been

standing out there for a half hour waiting for a woman who wasn't going to show.

Get the fucking hint, cowboy.

I walked back inside, trying to shake off the worry that something had happened to her. And beneath that, the sense that I had been rejected. Ridiculous. Totally ridiculous.

But there it was. This woman I didn't know. This woman who'd been in my life in this limited way for only, what... three mornings? She didn't show up and I missed her.

I missed my Morning Girl.

I put the tools in the beat-up lockbox in the corner of the first floor and snapped the lock closed.

In three hours I was supposed to meet Bea to empty out the bar. I smiled thinking about that woman, as I imagined most the men who met her did when they thought about her.

She wasn't my Morning Girl...but then, no one really was.

BEA

I WORE my old overalls and a red tank top. A clip held my hair off my forehead, and even though the work I was going to do was sweaty and dirty I couldn't resist my ruby-red lipstick and a swipe of mascara.

It was weird how nervous I was emptying everything out of the bar. I left the door open for him even though I knew it was early. He wasn't supposed to show up until after noon.

Ridiculous how nervous I was.

This morning at 7 a.m. I'd stood at the sliding glass door

out to my deck, my hand on the door, and forced myself not to go out there. It seemed mean knowing what he didn't know. And I was a lot of things but mean wasn't one of them.

But he'd waited for me. Shifting from leg to leg for close to a half hour.

He waited.

And that felt...huge. Strange. Sweet.

I cued my phone to the speaker and soon I had Kacey Musgraves blasting through the system. And after enough Kacey Musgraves blasting through the system, the nerves went away. Enough Kacey Musgraves at the right volume and I forgot I was a King.

The right Kasey Musgraves song, at the right volume, and I started to believe I was Kacey Musgraves.

The dried-out limes and lemons and oranges got dumped in the garbage, and I contemplated putting the cherries back in the jar but dumped them before I started to put the bottles into boxes.

I pulled two dusty, barely used crème de menthe bottles off the mirrored shelf and contemplated tossing those away with the lemons and lines.

"Hello?" someone yelled over "Step Off" and I didn't have to turn around to see my cowboy to know my cowboy was there.

My cowboy... That had to stop.

"Hey." I set the bottles down on the counter and turned Kasey down until I was myself again. "You're early,"

"Is that okay?" he asked. He stood just inside the door, and the sunlight coming through it behind him gave him a kind of halo. His face was shadowed but even from across the room I could smell he'd showered.

"Totally," I said. I found him hard to look at and I could

feel my heart pounding in my neck. This secret I was keeping took all the air out of the room. *Tell him*, I thought. *Tell him right now. Before you talk about anything else.*

He stepped out of the dusty murk around the door, each step bringing him into the brighter light of the bar. He wore a white shirt with faded lettering across the front, a pair of worn Levi's, and those boots of his.

"You sure are pretty," I said, because when I was uncomfortable I liked to make the ground uneven for everyone.

He smiled, a crooked, bashful thing that shouldn't seem genuine. It should seem cheeky and cheap and put on. "I did my hair," he joked, brushing his hand through the thick blond strands on his head, making it all stand up and glitter in the light.

"For me?" I asked.

"Who else?"

It was barely C+ flirtation; really, the most it deserved was a good eyeroll. But I blushed and looked away like a teenage girl made all rattley inside. And even as a teenage girl I hadn't been a person who got rattley. I was deeply uncomfortable being rattley.

"It looks different in the daylight. Smaller," he said, looking around the daylight wonder that was The Bar.

"Dirtier."

"That, too."

"Bars usually do."

"Do you want me to leave?" he asked.

"Leave? Why?"

"You...well...you kind of look uncomfortable. I don't want to make you uncomfortable."

"Not at all," I lied emphatically. "And you don't."

"Okay." He nodded as if glad that had been decided. "Where should I start?"

I shoved the booze in my hands into his hands. My pinky touched his finger. The finger he'd licked the come off. And both of us stood there for just a second, our fingers touching. And it was tiny, nothing. I could barely feel him there against my finger but somehow...I felt him. The touch of his finger against mine filled in all the blanks in my imagination. And there were so many. His skin was warm and rough. And I wanted more of it against mine.

This was why I didn't shake his hand the other day. It was dangerous.

Tell him.

"Cody, I should—"

"So, where do these go?" he asked, pulling the bottles out of my hands and breaking the contact.

"Those boxes." I pointed to the boxes behind him and he nodded, glancing down at the bottles.

"I guess you don't use crème de menthe all that often," he said, clearing the dust off the label with his thumb.

"Not all that many grasshopper orders around here."

"Those green drinks with the ice cream?" he said. "My mom loved them."

"Yeah?" There was something in his voice. A kind of fondness that made me smile.

"If she was home on a Friday she'd make a blender full of them. Give me some without the booze. They're pretty delicious."

"Well without the minty booze they're just ice cream."

"Mine were minty."

"Maybe she gave you the booze."

He laughed a little. "That wouldn't be all that surprising."

He put the bottles in the boxes and picked up a few

more from the bar that I'd taken off the mirrored shelves. "Kahlua," he said with another smile.

"Your mom have a thing for White Russians?" I asked.

"As a matter of fact..."

"Really?"

"She was...kind of a throwback, you know?" he said and began putting bottles in boxes faster than I was getting them off the shelves so I stepped up my work. "She was a stewardess. Worked a lot. She was...a real looker."

"And loved a sweet drink?"

"Loved them. Sweet drinks and Virginia Slims and hot pink nail polish. She smelled like hairspray and men's cologne."

"Men's cologne?"

"She liked sweet drinks and dangerous men." That smile faded.

"Well, who doesn't?" I said, because he seemed quiet and sad. I took a deep breath. "Look," I said. "There is something—"

"Are there more boxes?" he asked, changing the subject, no doubt because he was quiet and sad and embarrassed about being that way. He'd revealed too much, too soon. Conversations about mothers could do that. It was incredibly sweet. And I backed right off telling him about who we actually were to each other.

He was already embarrassed. I didn't need to compound it.

What a cowardly Bea King thing to do, a little voice said in my head. But I ignored that voice. I always had.

"In the back room." I jerked a thumb at the dark doorway to the left of the bar.

"I'll get them," he said and was gone before I could say more.

He came back with an arm full of flattened boxes.

"I had an idea," he said, setting the boxes down and starting to build them.

"Really?"

"You should do a retro drink menu," he said. "Grasshoppers and White Russians and Amaretto Stone Sours."

"You think someone is going to order those?"

"I don't know—those White Russians are real delicious. But, yeah, I think girls will. And boys will who want to hang out with those girls. And if you made it a thing."

"A thing?"

"Yeah. You know. A theme night."

"Cody," I said, my hands on my hips. "What do you know about theme nights?"

He grinned that grin that went right through me. The grin that said he'd seen some things in this world and he wouldn't mind seeing a few more. "A thing or two," he said. "You could do a whole retro thing. You dress up like you were the other day." Oh, I liked that. I liked that a lot. He'd noticed how I looked the other day and a warm blush climbed my body. "Or like that *Mad Men* show—"

"I do like a pencil skirt."

"Right."

"And a crinoline."

"I don't...know what that is."

"A thing that makes a skirt all poufy."

He shrugged. "It's an idea. Jack would probably go for it."

"Jack would totally go for it," I agreed, and could imagine the whole thing playing out. He'd get all wide-eyed and excited and he'd tell me to run with it, and the next thing I knew I'd be manager. And there'd be a hundred expectations on me and I'd fail all of them.

"But?" he asked.

"But what?"

"That silence of yours was a *but* silence—"

"Why are we talking about this?"

"We're not," he said.

"I'm just saying...I'm not in the position to be taking big ideas to Jack."

He shrugged and set the empty boxes on the stool. "I think Jack would do just about anything you told him to do."

Embarrassed, I shook my head and quickly changed the subject. "Cody, I've met you all of two times. I don't know how you'd get that idea when I don't even know your last name."

"McBride."

The name rang distant bells. "Cody McBride?"

"That's me. What's your—"

"Cody McBride. Why....?" I narrowed my eyes like that might help.

"What are you doing?"

I tilted my head. Like that might help.

He laughed and kept building boxes.

"Cody McBride. Cody McBride. Cody...I know you. Don't I?"

"Probably not. But my grandmother was Edna."

"Edna McBride! She made all the cakes!" Any special-occasion cake made in this town for a graduation, wedding, or birthday had been made by Edna. Nothing fancy, but delicious and decorated with flowers. Flowers no matter what. Someone could ask for a football on their cake and it would be a football made out of flowers.

"Yes, she did." He smiled down at the boxes. "But her real thing was pies. Did you ever have one of her pies?"

"No."

"They were like..." He shook his head. This sweet talkative cowboy was made speechless by his grandma's pies. "Nothing else I've ever had. Ever. That new bakery across the street, she makes cherry pies on Monday and they're good. They're close but they're not my grandmother's."

I did not expect to feel that warm little blast of pride. "That's...that's my sister," I said. "Sabrina's Sweet Things. Sabrina is my sister."

"No shit. She's a talented woman."

"No shit. But the question is—who are you, Cody McBride?" I squinted and tilted my head and he chuckled a little. It was a nice sound and the kind that made me want to tease him into making it again.

"No one special—"

"Rodeo!" I cried. "You were a senior when I was a freshman. Right? You left early to rodeo full-time."

"Jesus, how do you remember that?"

"You were kinda a big deal, Cody McBride." He'd walked the halls of school and the freshman cheerleaders and rally girls fell in his wake. The walls smoked where he leaned against them. He left an impression and we'd been in school together for roughly five minutes.

"That was a long time ago," he said quietly. Sad again.

What was it about sad men that made me crazy to make them smile? To comfort them in some way? I leaned against the bar, resting just right so he could get a good look down my shirt if he wanted. What was wrong with me that I'd give him that, just because he was sad?

My sister would tell me that was my thing. Giving myself away for pennies when I was worth millions but...there was something about Cody.

"You really were a very big deal," I said, remembering. He'd won some big competitions and had been doing local commercials for car dealerships. I lost track of him when Ronnie and I went to Austin.

"A long time ago." He caught himself looking down my shirt and quickly looked away. The tips of his ears went a bit pink.

Oh, honey, I thought. *You've seen so much more.* But now was clearly not the time to talk to him about that.

"I competed for about eight years."

"And then what?"

"I stopped."

"Why?"

This time when he looked at me he wasn't blushing and he didn't look down my shirt. He was pissed. "Do you really not know? Or is this some kind of make-conversation thing?"

"Make conversation? No, if we were making conversation I'd ask you about your sex life."

"Then what is this?"

I shrugged. "Getting to know you."

Somehow, we both seemed slightly taken aback by my words. Which wasn't anything new for me. Words often come out of my mouth that I hadn't planned or thought about.

"I got hurt," he finally said.

"When?"

"Six months ago."

"I'm sorry."

"Me, too."

"That's why you limp?" I was prying and that was crappy, but I couldn't seem to stop. And he was answering, kind of like he couldn't stop.

He nodded. "Destroyed my knee. Total blow-out. Doctors said I'd never compete again. They said I needed to be grateful that I was walking."

"Are you? Grateful." Because there was something in the way he said those words that did not seem the slightest bit grateful. I knew anger when I heard someone pretending it didn't exist.

"I wasn't and now I'm...trying."

"How is that going?"

"Some days better than others. Today is a good day."

Oh, cowboy, that smile is gonna get you in trouble.

"What happened?" I asked. "The accident?" He was silent for so long I felt my face get hot. "Sorry, you don't have to...I don't mean to pry."

"Well, it's hardly prying since you can go on YouTube and watch five minutes of video."

I would never do that. Wouldn't want to. But the way he said it indicated he'd watched that five minutes of video lots of times.

My heart just about broke for him.

"Bulldogging competition. That's when the rider—"

"Steer wrestling," I said. "I know the lingo." Texas girls who had an eye for rodeo boys caught on fast.

"Right." The smile was a quick flash on his face. "Well, I misjudged the steer and he changed course last minute, and I tried to save myself and my horse but it was too late, and when I jumped, my foot got tangled and I ended up pulling her down with me. The steer dragged me and by that time I'd shattered my knee cap and my femur."

"That sounds awful."

"They said I was lucky it wasn't my pelvis. My horse broke two legs."

"They put her down?"

"I begged them not to."

"I'm sorry."

"Me, too."

"Do you miss it?"

He was still building boxes, but I'd given up making it seem like I was working at all.

He opened his mouth, shut it, and shook his head. I didn't think he was going to answer and I certainly wasn't going to push. I turned away and started pulling more bottles off the shelf behind the bar.

"I miss being good at something," he said, and I stilled, looking up to catch a glimpse of him in the mirror. "I miss how simple my life used to be. I miss the way my body felt—like I could do anything. I miss how it felt to win. I miss..." He stopped shook his head, and then looked up and caught my eye in the mirror. I startled as if he'd caught me. But he only smiled. "You don't want to know all that."

"Sure I do," I said.

We were quiet for a second. I was waiting for him to say something and it was growing obvious as he built boxes that he was done talking.

Now, I thought. *Now. Do it now. Just say the words.*

8

I *know you're doing the work next door and I know that*
because I'm the woman you've been watching on the deck
every morning. I watched you lick come off your hand.
Your eyes make me come so hard I can barely walk after.

I imagined he'd be flabbergasted for a second and then
he'd be angry. And he'd cross the room with long strides,
just a tiny hitch on that injured leg. And he'd flip that lock
closed and when he turned, his face would be still and careful, but the tips of his ears would be hot.

You lied to me, he would say.

No, I would say, backing away from him. *No. I didn't lie, I*
just didn't tell you.

You know what happens to women who lie to me? he'd ask,
and scared and turned on I would only shake my head.

And maybe he'd tell me to take off my clothes and
maybe he'd tell me to lean over the bar. And maybe he'd
bring that big wide palm down against the bare cheeks of
my ass. Or maybe he'd drop to his knees behind me.

"What's your name?" he asked, snapping me out of my
little daydream and the moment to tell him was over,

burned up in my fantasy. But now I was all hot and bothered under my overalls thinking about him eating me out from behind.

"What?"

"Just wondering what your name is."

Right. My name. My name would put an end to all of this, too. My name would change the way he looked at me. My name had that kind of power.

"Bea."

He smiled at me. "We went to school together, but I don't remember you and I think I would remember you."

"You were four years older than me. And I was...awkward."

"I don't believe it for a minute."

"Well, the class pictures would make a believer out of you."

"You want me to box those up?" he asked, pointing to all the glasses I'd stacked on the bar. I didn't even remember doing that, lost in that fantasy.

"Sure."

"Do you have paper or something? To wrap them?"

"No. In fact, I think the best thing for these glasses is if they all broke."

He laughed. "I wish I had known you," he said. "In high school. It would have been nice to know you."

Oh, my god. I wanted to strip off my clothes right then and there. I wanted to push him back against the door and kiss that beautiful sweet and sad mouth. I wanted my breasts to put a smile on his face and I wanted his dick to put a smile on mine and...

"Yeah," I said. "Probably would have improved my high school experience to have you as a friend."

That made him laugh. "It would improve my experience now," he said, "to have friends."

"You always had a ton of friends," I said.

"Did I?"

"That's how I remember it."

He laughed a little bitterly. "I think it was more fun being around me when I was winning."

"You got hurt and they left?"

"They weren't really friends, I guess."

God. The guy had been hurt. Was lucky to be walking and all his friends had left him. It was gross. "I'll be your friend," I said.

"Yeah?" Again with that half grin, that charming curl. Like there was a joke and we were both in on it.

"Yeah."

I walked around the bar and held out my hand. I'd avoided touching him because of those blank spaces in my imagination. Because my imagination clearly didn't need any help building up incredibly deviant daydreams about this man. I'd avoided touching him because there were rules I was trying to live by. Because I was a new Bea King.

And I wasn't comforting sad cowboys with my body these days.

And I wasn't being comforted by sad cowboy's bodies these days.

We shook hands, and even though I was trying not to feel it, the touch of his sizzled up my arm. It sizzled up my arm and across my shoulders and down into my breasts. My belly.

I sucked in a breath and so did he. Like he was feeling it, too. Like I wasn't alone with this sizzle and this kind of gasping breathlessness.

This sudden, delicious awareness.

I knew. I knew it would be like this. Like he would be like this.

Like we would.

Lock the door, I thought in a fever. *Tell me to lock the door and than shove me against it. Let me run my hand down your chest, to the front of your jeans. Let me touch you. And I will let you touch the fuck out of me.*

He squeezed my hand and I squeezed his back. His thumb brushed against the fleshy muscle at the base of my thumb and my lungs became too small to pull in a breath. I liked how small my hand was in his. How big his was around mine. It made me think of his body and mine, and the beautiful and perfectly compatible differences between them.

"Bea," he whispered, and his arm contracted, like his biceps spasmed and pulled me closer. Not a lot. Just a tiny stumbling step. I looked into his eyes. Green. Like a Mountain Dew bottle. He looked at my mouth, which parted on a breath I didn't plan.

None of this was coy. All of it was real and I hadn't felt anything like this...maybe ever.

He dropped my hand and took a step back. Putting double the distance between us. So I did, too. Soon almost the entirety of the bar was between us and I still couldn't quite catch my breath.

"Bea," he said. "I don't...I don't want this to sound weird or be...weird."

"It already is."

"You are so beautiful. Just the most beautiful."

"None of that is weird."

"My gran died. My career...died. I'm broke. Like, broker than broke. I'm barely keeping my head above water."

"And?"

"And I'm scared of pulling anyone down with me. And..." He smiled, his eyes walking all over my face, and then he laughed, a humphy, breathy thing that told me a pretty good story about his frustration.

And his desire.

Because I had the same breathy, humphy laugh in my throat.

"I don't have a lot of friends right now. And I think...I think I'd like to have you as friend."

"And you think fucking each other would mess that up."

"Has it ever not messed it up for you?"

I shook my head. Because he was right. Friends with benefits always ended without a friend and without benefits.

"Good point," I said and turned away from him.

"Did I make it weird?"

"Nope," I said. "You let me down very gently."

"You really are so beautiful."

"Trust me, Cody. I know."

I winked at him and took my place back behind the bar feeling a war rage in my brain.

I had to tell him that I was the woman on the deck. I had to.

But then that would be over.

And now, because I'd waited, the friendship might be over. Because while none of what he said had made it weird between us, the truth about who we were to each other in the early morning sunlight would totally make it weird.

And I hadn't lied. I wanted a friend, too.

Fuck. And I hadn't told him I was a King.

Oh, my god. I could fuck something up twenty different ways without even trying.

"Bea? You okay?" he asked.

"Fine. I'm just...how do we knock this down?" I skated right past that moment that I needed to tell the truth about all of it. About everything. I pointed to the bar. In the mirror behind it I could see him looking at me. Watching me.

And it made nothing easier that he was checking me out. His desire completely unguarded. We could be friends, but he wanted me.

Which made me feel a little better about wanting him.

None of it made me feel better about lying to him.

"I've got a hammer next door," he said.

"A big one?"

"Couple of them."

"Sounds good."

I watched in the mirror as he walked toward the door. As sweet as that man's face was, the view of him walking away was just as fine. But then he stopped in the doorway. Put his hand up for the door and then stopped. Turned back toward me and then back toward the door.

"Cody? You all right?"

"Do you know...ah...do you know who lives next door?"

My heart literally stopped in my chest. It was so fast. So sudden I saw stars. "Next door?"

"In the apartment upstairs."

I bit my lip. Realized how hard it was to be different than who I was. How selfish I was in my heart and how I didn't want to screw this up. How I wanted to be friends with this man and I wanted to keep getting naked in front of this man and how I would lie to get what I wanted.

"No idea."

9

C ODY

I WALKED out of Jack's bar covered in dust, my shoulders screaming from the repeated slamming of a sledgehammer against the wall.

And my cheeks hurt. Because Bea was just that way. She was the kind of woman...the kind of person and friend who put a smile on a person's face. And god, she'd worked hard.

She must be sore. If I was sore...she must be really hurting.

If I was the me of five years ago—fuck, seven months ago —I would go back in there. Rub her shoulders, take her to wherever she lived, and run her a bath. Pour her a glass of whatever she wanted.

But I was the me of now, which meant that I said good night, gave her a smile, and walked out.

The me of now was lame.

My back pocket buzzed, and since I never got calls these days, I practically jumped.

Glory Rehabilitation Center.

Shit. I couldn't bounce another check with them. I was on thin ice as it was.

"Hello?"

"Cody McBride" A woman asked. A woman I hadn't heard before. She sounded like an accountant, too. Slightly disapproving. I could hear clicking of computer keys on her end. I was sure, despite how impossible it was, that she could see into my overdrawn bank account.

Jack was going to have to give me an advance on that raise he promised.

"Yeah."

"I'm calling to discuss next steps with you," she said.

"What steps?"

"Well, Bonnie has completed her rehabilitation."

"Right. I talked to Dr. Whittaker last week."

"And now I'm calling to see if you'd like to keep Bonnie here. Or if you have plans to move her."

"Move her." I laughed, suddenly imagining Bonnie in Gran's living room.

"We have the facility for her to stay here but I just need to talk to you about payment."

"How...much does it cost?" I asked. I closed my eyes and prayed because I had no place for Bonnie and it would be amazing if she could stay there.

"Four thousand a month. Food, board—"

I laughed. I laughed so hard. Four thousand was just slightly less than what I'd been paying for her rehab and care.

"Mr. McBride?"

"I'm sorry," I said. "But no, ma'm. I can't keep her there."

"Okay," she said, and again there was computer clicking and clacking at her end of the phone. "You have four days until you need to find her other accommodations."

Four days. What in the world was I going to be able to do in four days?

Of course, I was in Texas. There had to be twenty places offering boarding services within spitting distance. I had just had to find them.

I looked down at my phone. My thumb of its own accord pulling up Charlie's number.

Charlie would know. He might even help. Fuck, who was I kidding? He'd fall over himself to help. He'd find out where I was and be here as fast as he could.

And I wasn't going to do that to Charlie.

Not again.

Tuesday I was supposed to be framing the joint bar space between the two buildings before the crews came in next week, but so far I'd spent most of the morning on my phone.

I had twenty calls out and eighteen of them were coming in all at the same time. None of them had good news.

Places were full. Places were closed.

"You're that rodeo guy," one woman said. "The kid that got hurt—"

"Lots of us get hurt, m'am."

"Yeah...but you're Edna McBride's grandboy."

I swallowed. "I am."

"Yeah. You know what happened the last time I had one of you rodeo hotshots in my place? It was party central every weekend."

"I won't actually be there."

That made the woman on the other end of the phone pause. "What? You won't be here on the weekends?"

"I won't be there ever."

"Why?"

"Does it matter, if I'm paying the bill?"

Her silence spoke volumes. "You know something, son," she said. "I don't think you're our kind of people."

"Sorry?"

"We don't have any room."

And then she hung up. I stared down at the phone, its screen gone blank.

That was the truth of things these days. I wasn't anyone's kind of people. Not anymore. I used to be all kinds of people's kind of people and now look at me.

I heard, in some kind of deep, dark corner of my brain, the swish of a deck door open. The bark of an excited dog.

Jesus—I tapped my phone. It was five after seven.

On any other day, in any other time of my life, the way I practically ran out the back door of that building to my spot under the tree beside the debris pile would have been embarrassing.

Today I couldn't care. I just didn't want to miss her.

I got to my spot on the other side of that tree and for a second I didn't see her. The leaves and branches of that oak tree seemed bigger today. They covered more of her. The rain from last week doing its job.

"Sorry," I said. "I was...busy."

She stepped sideways and I saw her more clearly. Well, her legs.

Jesus. Fuck.

She wore red heels and black stockings that ended at the tops of her thighs. I couldn't see what else she had on but that was enough. That was....more than enough.

I was ready for whatever she was going to show me. But she just stood there. Her legs, endless and strong looking, spread wide like she was conquering something. And then, suddenly, she turned toward her door, like she was going to leave.

"Please," I said, stepping forward, my knee screaming at the sudden movement. My knee did not like sudden movement. I could see more of her from this angle, which made me think there were places back here where I could probably see all of her. Even her face.

I was going to do absolutely nothing to seek out those places.

"I was busy on the phone. It's important. Otherwise I would have been here." I shook my head. I felt ridiculous. Desperate. Like I'd felt in the eighth grade trying to get Monica Blakely to keep doing what she was doing with her hand down my pants. But I couldn't seem to stop myself. "Please don't leave."

She didn't leave. But she didn't sit. Either. And the moment hung, us inside of it.

Back in the day—my good old days—rodeo had been like this. Me and the horse. The steer I was going to wrestle. When it was good, when the day was right. It was just like this.

Like we breathed the same air. Like we had the same heartbeat.

"I like this," I said. "These mornings. I...love them. But I have to tell you they're going to end."

I knew she could hear me but she didn't move. She didn't sit in her chair.

God, I really wanted her to sit in the chair. I wanted her to spread those legs with the red shoes and the black silk stockings...

"There are going to be more people here,' I said. "Next week. So, we can't...you know. Keep doing this. We have five days," I said. "Four, I guess."

She sat down in her chair and I saw the tops of those stockings. The black underwear, the sweet fleshy curve of her inner thigh. She had a birthmark there. A small dark circle on the inside of her leg. I hadn't noticed it before. All the things she'd shown me and this felt unbearably intimate.

I had a flash of Bea in the bar the other day, when she bent over and I saw that pink lace above her jeans. I didn't want to think of Bea right now. Or the difference between my Morning Girl's consent and Bea's unknowing flashing of something private. So I shook Bea out of my head and I concentrated on my Morning Girl as she put her hands on her knees and ran them up her legs to that beautiful sweet spot. That secret place.

"I'm so fucking lucky," I said. Because I couldn't not say it. "So fucking lucky you show me this."

I ran my hand up my own legs, to my aching cock under my zipper and made a move to undo my belt. But she held up her hand and I stopped.

Like she'd yanked my leash I stopped.

"Just me," she said. I almost complained. Asked why. Said no. But then she slipped her fingers under that black silk and I didn't care anymore. I could come in my pants and I couldn't give a shit.

I watched her play with her clit. I watched her slip a finger deep inside her pussy and then add another one, and gritted my teeth and kept my hands off my cock.

She gasped and made this low growling sound in her throat, and I felt the orgasm bite down on my neck without even touching myself. Fuck, this hadn't happened in years. Coming in my pants without even a pillow to rub up against.

She lifted those fingers that had been deep in her pussy and I imagined her putting those fingers in her mouth.

I closed my eyes, bit my lip, and made fists so hard I swear to god I could have broken my hands. But still I felt that orgasm rippling through me. I tried to think of baseball. The pain of a shattered kneecap. Charlie's face over the side of my hospital bed.

None of it worked.

She groaned and laughed, and I opened my eyes so I wouldn't miss a second of that woman's orgasm. Her skin, the skin I could see, was flushed, rosy, and splotchy. She was gasping. Shaking in that chair. And then...slowly she was still. Her fingers slipped out of her body. Her legs closed.

The moment over.

I sat there, a wet spot growing on my jeans, and slowly she got up. She stepped from her chair to the door and I wanted to tell her to stop. I wanted to tell her to wait. To bend down so I could see her face. I wanted to ask her to invite me up.

I kept my mouth shut and she walked back inside.

10

B EA

I WAITED until I was sure he was gone. I watched out my front window from behind the shades as he put his tools in his truck. There was no way for me to hear the tailgate getting slammed shut, but I swore I could hear it. I even flinched.

But then he stood there for a second, his arms braced wide across the rusty metal. The R in the Ram had fallen off, leaving only a dirty outline. He rolled his shoulders, the muscles under his shirt shifting. I wondered if he was hurt. I knew he was stressed out about something. He'd said that. He'd told me...

Or he told the morning girl. The distinction felt clear.

Look up, I thought. *See me. Please, look up. I'm right here.*

But all he did was fish his keys out of his pocket, walk around to the driver's-side door, get in, and drive away.

Louise barked. She'd climbed up on the table like she knew I wouldn't stop her. Like she knew I didn't have the will or the power.

"Stop judging me," I muttered but she only barked more. "It's a week," I said. "One week. And then it's over."

He'd made it clear he didn't want to date me, and I couldn't date him. So...we had this. The morning. For one more week. Well, four days.

But who was counting.

Four days and then...over. I could live with that.

I dressed in my scrubbiest scrub clothes because I had unleashed a beast and I was going to clean up the bar after the work from yesterday. And then I was thinking I'd go after the kitchen if I still had steam.

I gave Thelma a bone. It was my new way to try and keep her from destroying all my shoes. One delicious, super-expensive marrow-filled bone a day. I gave Louise a scrub under the chin while she gave me some serious side-eye and I went downstairs.

The plan was to clean and work until I didn't think about the four mornings I had left.

CLEANING WAS pure Steve Earle time. I needed Steve Earle and The Dukes telling me they'd promise me anything to get through the gunge and the muck, and Steve Earle led me to EmmyLou and I wondered for the like the eight hundredth time how EmmyLou and I weren't best friends. It just seemed ridiculous that we didn't hang out all the time.

"Hello?" someone yelled over "Two More Bottles of Wine," like that wasn't practically my motto. (See, Emmy-Lou? We were meant to be.)

"Yeah!" I yelled back. I had finished cleaning off the bar,

taking a minute to admire Cody's work framing out the big open window between what would be the two spaces. And had moved on to the kitchen. I was pulling up the black mats in there and what I found underneath them made me want to die.

"Jesus, girl, what are you doing?" Cody stood in the doorway and pressed his hands against the frame above his head. It was such a guy thing to do. Women didn't stand like that. It made my goddamn mouth water.

"What does it look like?" I asked, staring down at the black mats and the gunk underneath.

"Like you're trying to get a staph infection."

I laughed and dropped the mats. "You're a funny man, Cody."

"No one has ever accused me of that."

He rubbed the back of his neck, a bashful cowboy in clean blue jeans. I didn't even try not to feel good about this morning. Making this man come in his pants like a teenager.

This power was wicked and it went to my head like a shot of grain alcohol.

We were staring at each other. Each of us from the corners of our eyes, like we could hide what we were doing. *Foolish*, I thought.

Dangerous.

I yanked hard on the black mats and they curled right up, making a squelching sound.

"Here," he said. "Let me help you." He grabbed one end and I grabbed the other. "Let's take them out back."

I walked backward out the door and around the edge of the deck to the dumpster.

"Count of three?" I said.

"Three," he said and just hefted the whole gross thing

up and into the bin. The Strong Cowboy Show was a good one.

"Thank you," I said, wiping my hands on my jeans.

"My pleasure."

I made a point of not looking next door, like I was completely unaware of the oak tree and the building behind my back. He, however, was looking up at that deck like he couldn't help himself.

She's not there, Romeo. She's right in front of you.

"What are you doing here?" I hadn't been expecting him. We'd demo'd the wall and he'd framed it up this morning. He wasn't supposed to be back.

"I don't know, I figured the way you were yesterday you'd be back at it today."

"The way I was yesterday? What does that mean?"

"My Gran would have called you a dog with a bone."

I arched an eyebrow at him, not appreciating the canine comparison.

"*I* would say you were a woman with a mission."

"Well, the bar is closed today so it only makes sense to clean this place up."

"Right. And I just thought you might want some help."

Dammit. I mean...*dammit.*

"What would your Gran say about turning down free help?"

"Only fools would do it."

"And I'm no fool." Only that really wasn't true. Like, at all. I was more foolish every minute I spent with this guy. Ever second in his company was like playing with fire. "Follow me."

I led him back into the kitchen, which was greasy and small and made practically no sense. I wasn't going to do anything to the equipment. Or the food in the freezers and fridge.

But everything else was fair game.

"Can I ask you something?" Cody said as we threw all the red plastic baskets Jack served his food in into the garbage bin. Half of them were melted. Most of them were broken. All of them were gross.

"Depends."

"Why don't you want to be manager?"

"Of this place?"

"Yeah. You seem to like it."

"I do. I like it a lot, actually. It's a good bar. Good people. Jack is—"

"The best," Cody supplied in a way that made me believe he would not be listening to any gossip about Jack.

"Yes," I said quietly. "He really is."

"So? Why don't you manage?"

I'd moved on from the red plastic baskets to the wax paper we lined them with. I tossed the open box out. Left the unopened box.

"I just feel like the second someone expects more out of me, wants more from me, that's when the disappointment starts, you know? That's when they find out I'm not who they thought I was. And worse, it's when I find out I'm not who *I* thought I was."

"What do you mean?"

Oh, man, I had about a zillion stories I could share.

"My sister and I are close, you know. Real close. And this whole thing happened with her husband years ago. He, like...crushed her into dust, and I swooped in and picked her up and I got her to safety and I was, like... amazing."

We were cleaning the stainless-steel shelves over the

fryer and it was a disgusting mix of things up there. Mostly stacks of to-go cups the staff used to drink Jack and Cokes.

"Super Sister."

"Hold that thought, cowboy. Because we just get settled in Austin and I have to go back home. Because I have this shit-bag boyfriend at the time, and I'm so worried about him and what he's going to think."

"What did he think?"

"That some redhead he met at a bar should suck his dick." I didn't know what I was tossing in the garbage now. But all of it went. Everything on that shelf got tossed.

"What?" His outrage was sweet. It was a nice little balm on an old wound that refused to scab over.

"Yeah. I walked into his apartment to find him getting a blow job from some stranger."

"What...what did you do?"

"Well, I'd like to say that I realized he wasn't worth my time and I turned right around and left."

"But you didn't."

"I didn't. I got in a fight with the woman, who actually beat the crap out of me—"

"You're...you're joking."

"Wish I was. She gave me black eye and split my lip. I got out of there with absolutely no dignity. But...." I put my finger up. "I went back the next day and grabbed my things. And I stole his baseball signed by Nolan Ryan. And his dog."

"His dog? Remind me not to cross you." He laughed. Which was the point, really. But none of it was funny.

"Well, I took his dog." His dog was Louise, but I wasn't telling Cody that. The old boyfriend had treated Louise like she was a problem when she was a blessing. "Anyway, his dog always liked me better. In the middle of the night I ran right back to Austin, so I could live with my sister. In the five years we spent there she discovered she's all kind of super-woman and I made another shitty choice about a man. I'd made some money off the sale of the baseball, so I decided to open a bar with this guy. Then he stole all my money, destroyed my credit, and disappeared, leaving me with a partially renovated bar and thousands of dollars in debt."

His silence was embarrassing. This whole stupid thing was embarrassing. Which is why I liked to keep the conversations light. Easy. And never about me.

I grabbed the full garbage bags but he took them out of my hands and headed for the door. I stood in the doorway and watched him, feeling raw and embarrassed.

"No wonder you're gun-shy," he said quietly when he came back in. I did not look at him. Refused to. Instead I opened up another heavy-duty trash bag and went after the condiments.

"It's like I have these moments, you know. These moments when I have all my shit together and I get to be a hero."

"I get that."

"And then I wake up and I'm not a hero. I'm Bea fucking King and all I do is disappoint people."

He stared at me, an old bottle of ketchup falling into the garbage from his suddenly limp hand.

"Bea...fucking...King?"

Oh, shit. Did I say that? I did. I said that.

"See what I mean?" I muttered.

"You're Bea King and you're working...here?"

"Girl's gotta work."

"Not if she's a King!" He laughed. "I can't believe I didn't put this together before now."

Yeah, me too.

And this, God, this was what I'd wanted to avoid with

him. It wasn't the money that made things weird. It was the perception of the money. It was what people thought I should be. Or want.

How the hell could they so clearly know who I was supposed to be, when I didn't have a clue?

Weirdly...I mean, *so* weirdly, I felt tears burn in my eyes and it had been years since I'd cried over my mistakes.

"Hey." He touched my wrist, which filled me with sparks and a kind of anguished embarrassment that he could affect me that way, even when I felt so shitty.

I wiped at my eyes and walked out of the kitchen. For no good reason but to get away. To get a breath that didn't smell like that sour floor. A breath that he wasn't watching.

"Bea," he said, following me into the better-lit bar. Dust sparkled in the sunlight that came in through the dusty windows. I should clean those. "Listen. I'm sorry. I...hell, I know what it's like to be on the other end of someone else's assumptions. I should know better and I am real sorry if I hurt your feelings."

"You didn't do anything but say what everyone else says about me." It was so easy to forgive anyone but myself.

"Yeah, and I was just starting to think I wasn't like everyone else." Oh, the sweetness of those words. I knew he meant friendship, but still, they were just so bittersweet.

"Thanks," I said with a big sigh and a smile that wasn't faked.

"Bea King, huh?" he asked.

"Bea King."

"I should have put two and two together when you said Sabrina was your sister."

I shrugged. "She's my half sister and she changed her name when she married Garrett. But...yeah. She's a King, too." The last thing I wanted to talk about was Sabrina and

Garrett and all their happiness. "Hey. You said you were busy. What's going on?"

"Busy?"

"Yeah, you—" I had that cold feeling from the top of my head. Shock and dread. The sensation of having jumped off a cliff.

He hadn't told me that.

He told the other girl. The other me.

11

"I don't know, you seemed stressed...when you came in," I said quickly. A terrible cover-up.

"Did I?" He rubbed a hand over his face. "I just have...a thing."

"I told you about my thing. Give me a shot. Maybe I can help."

"Really, you can only help me if you have a stable. And room for my horse. And maybe some loose rules regarding when and how often I visit."

"Yep, yep, and I don't think I care how much you visit."

He blinked at me and I felt the reverse of what I usually felt about being a King. Instead of dread, I felt the power of the name. The money. And in this case—the land. That awful house I hated with all my heart. And the stables I loved.

In my life I was never the kind of person people went to with their problems. Unless they wanted to drink them away for a few hours. The lucky few got to fuck them away for a few hours with me. But to solve problems? Yeah, I wasn't the King Sister for that. That was Ronnie's job.

"I'm not kidding," I told him. "I can take you out to the stables right now."

"Wait." He shook his head, his handsome face scrunched. "You're talking about The King's Land Stables?"

"Yeah. We don't have as many horses as we used to. Oscar is still there." I remembered something that Ronnie had said about an RV and Galveston, but that wasn't happening now. And even if Oscar left, there were still a few guys working.

It felt like, if it was required of me, I'd move back to that awful house and take care of the horse on my own.

Because of this feeling it gave me.

Because he was my friend.

"I can pay," he said, like it mattered. To him, anyway.

"Sure," I said, because it didn't matter to me at all. But I understood his pride. "You want to go check it out?"

"The King family stables?" He smiled at me. "Are you joking?"

"No."

"Fuck. Yes. I heard the stables are as big as the house."

"As big as the house before my stepmom built all the wings onto it. The original house and the stables were the same size. Which, yeah, is pretty big."

Oh, god, the delight. The happiness that came with making him happy. Was this how my sister felt all the damn time, every time she helped me out? Every time she jumped in to fix my problems?

No wonder she couldn't stop. It was addictive.

"Yeah, come on. We can go."

I glanced at my watch and then around the bar and was about to say *fuck it* and leave now. We could roll down all the windows in my Jeep and let the sun beat down on our faces. And maybe, drunk on sunshine and problem solving, we'd stop feeling like friendship was a safer bet than getting naked and sweaty. And we'd get naked and sweaty.

Bad idea. Really. Bad idea. But...still. It was there. The wanting him.

He was impossible not to want. And some terrible, insidious part of me, some needy, sad wanton part of me— wanted him to want me.

To want me as much as he wanted the naked girl on the deck.

"Let's put in one more hour," he said, proving he was a better person. Which made me want him more. "Finish the worst of the kitchen. What do you say?"

"Sure," I said. I would say yes. Yes over and over again. To whatever this man wanted. "One more hour."

CODY

THIS FELT RIDICULOUS. It felt like a dream. The sun was shining down on my head. Bonnie might have a place to stay and the woman driving the Jeep smelled like fresh laundry and flowers and sweat.

The sweat part was pretty hot.

"I've never been out here," I said over the wind.

"To The King's Land?" she asked. After we'd put in another hour at the bar, we'd both gone home to shower and reconvened back at the bar.

Her hair was pulled back and she'd wrapped some kind of head scarf around it. With the sunglasses she was wearing she looked like a 1940s bombshell. She looked like the kind of woman who'd never be with me. The women I pulled as a rodeo guy were, at times, just as classy and elegant and beautiful, but they tended to be mirrors, reflecting back whatever I wanted.

Bea was a hundred percent her own person. A mirror for no man.

And fucking rich. Like *rich* rich.

"You're not missing much," she said. "The house is awful. But the stables are nice. Your horse will like it."

My horse. Bonnie. If you'd told me at any time in my life that my horse would be stabled out at The King's Land... well, I'd have called you a liar.

Outside the window the world was kind of blonde—dry and brittle. Summer in Texas.

"I can pay you." I said it again. And I wasn't sure why.

"Hey," she said, glancing over at me with her bright turquoise cat's-eye glasses. "Is this going to be weird now?"

"What?"

"That I'm a King. That I have money. Is it going to be weird now? Because we were friends and that was kind of fun for me, and I don't want it to stop."

"Am I being weird?" I asked.

"Yeah. And I don't like it."

"Well, you have to give me a second to wrap my head around the fact that the bartender at my friend's bar is richer than god."

"Don't exaggerate," she said. "It's not funny."

"I have a question." I turned a little to face her. "Why are you working? Why does it seem like this money bums you out? Why—"

"Why aren't I happy?" she asked. "Because being a King has never really made me happy. And I'd give up all this money tomorrow. Tomorrow, if I could just—" she blew out a long breath "—figure out what I'm supposed to do with my life."

The wind whistled through the Jeep and I wasn't sure if she was going to say anything else.

"What do you want to do?" I asked her.

"What do you want to do?" she shot back.

Rodeo.

The answer came like it always did, swift and sudden. A punch to the stomach. A slap to the head.

I had to get used to a new answer. Charlie's thing was always about how making a new habit took thirty days. *Thirty days to change your life, kid.* He'd always say that to me with a big fat cigar hanging out of his mouth.

"I think, right now, I'm happy doing what I'm doing," I said. "It's just taking some getting used to." For months I'd hidden in my gran's house, afraid...of everything. Angry at the world. And then I got a job out at the Bruns build south of town which was fine. Good. But then Jack gave me that job doing demo, and I met Bea and everything felt different.

"You don't feel like you're supposed to want more?" she asked.

"Why?"

"I just...always feel like I'm supposed to want more. I'm a King, you know. My sister is out there making a difference in women's lives. Sabrina was on freaking TV and now she's got that damn bakery that's lined up out the door. There's no way I'm supposed to be happy being the dive bar queen."

"I don't think there's rules about it."

Bea laughed. "You haven't met Ronnie."

"I was the top-earning all-around champion for two years straight," I said. "I had endorsement deals, ate dinner with politicians and musicians and movie stars. Slept in hotels with king-size beds."

"And?"

"It can be hard to let go of it. But I'm trying."

It was surprising telling the truth. Like saying the words made them closer to being true.

She pulled through the gate, turned a dusty corner, and through a copse of trees there was a mansion.

"Jesus," I said, a little awed.

She laughed and parked in front of the mansion. "It's ugly, isn't it?"

I looked at her like she'd lost her mind. "It's beautiful. Really pretty." I'd expected something wild and ostentatious, but it was a big brick house. With white columns and lots of windows.

She tilted her head like she was hoping to get a different view. "You think?"

"I do."

"We're figuring out what to do with the place," she said. "None of us want it."

We stepped out of the Jeep under the bright blue sky and the air smelled like pure Texas—sunlight and dust and trees in the distance.

"I'll show you the stables," she said, stepping across the gravel parking area to the field beside the house and I followed. The stables were bright red with pretty turrets. Flapping white flags on the top of them. Like it was a castle.

The King's Land Stables had a top-notch reputation. If you wanted a fast quarter horse you came here. You wanted top-shelf working horses, you came here. Deana McKenzie, the number-one-ranked barrel racer, got her horse here.

It blew my mind that Bonnie could be living here.

There was a man leading a pretty Appaloosa out of the doors toward one of the many corrals and fields. The scene was so familiar it squeezed my heart.

"So," she said as we stepped into the dark of the barn.

The smell...God, the smell. Horse shit and hay and animals. The oil they used on the saddles.

Was this ever not going to hurt?

I stepped back, out of the stables. And breathed through my mouth.

"This looks great," I said. "I mean, Bonnie won't know what hit her—"

As soon as I said that stupid joke I wanted to eat my words.

"You don't want to see where she'll be? Meet Oscar?"

"Do you trust Oscar?"

"With my whole heart."

"Sounds great." I had to turn my back on the stables, look out at that house so I could keep breathing. "How...how much do I owe you?"

"Cody?" She ducked around to see my face, but I started walking away. I smiled, feeling like I might cry. Again. This is why I didn't go see her at the rehab facility. This is why I had to walk away and stay away. Because I couldn't get better. I couldn't feel better, move on, whatever. I couldn't do any of that if I was still walking into the places that reminded me of everything I'd lost.

"Hey," she said, and her hand touched my elbow. I jumped just slightly at the electric sizzle of the contact. The heat of her fingers I could feel through my T-shirt. "Cody?"

She slid her hand from my elbow to my shoulder and I followed the movement with all my concentration. I leaped onto her touching me, threw myself away from my grief and my fucking freak-out and just latched onto her.

"You okay?" she asked.

"Fine."

"Why are you lying?"

"Because I need it to be true."

"Okay," she breathed. "Hold on. Brace yourself."

"Why?"

She slid her arm over my shoulder, and then her other arm came around my other shoulder and the soft, tender skin of the inside of her elbows touched my neck. She stepped closer and closer until her chest touched mine. Her breasts... Fuck. God. Her breasts and then her hips, and my hands remembered what to do. They touched her waist, cupped that tensile heat with their palms, torn in that place between pulling her closer and pushing her away.

"Friends hug," she said, her breath in my ear, down the back of my shirt. She gave me goose bumps, like I was a child. And something about her made me *feel* young. Less jaded. Less...used and forgotten. Something about her hugging me made me feel new.

"We're not breaking any rules in the just friends handbook."

"Well, in that case," I said, and I pulled her to me with all my strength and I didn't so much as hug her as cling to her.

"I had a horse," she said. "As a kid. Tinkerbell."

"That's a great name."

"It was. And I loved her. We rode in some shows but we were terrible. Tink just wanted to eat apples and I just wanted to braid her mane."

"What happened?" I asked, because underneath the joke was something sad.

"Cancer. She was four. We had to put her down."

"I'm sorry."

"I know...tell me about your horse." She rested her head on my shoulder, her bony little chin finding some spot in the joint that didn't hurt.

"Bonnie," I said. And maybe it was easier because she

wasn't looking at me with those eyes. I couldn't see any pity there. I just felt the warm press of her all along my lonely body. "Her name is Bonnie and I had her for three years. She was...she was the most expensive thing I ever bought, you know? She was this beautiful, sleek, fast, strong beauty, and she was going to take my career to the next level. That's what Charlie said—"

"Charlie?"

I shook my head because I didn't want to talk about Charlie. I hadn't even meant to mention him.

"I took one look at her and...I just knew. I just knew she was mine. She knew which way to cut before I did, she knew when to pour it on, when to ease up. And she trusted me. Like, she would have jumped over a cliff if I made her think that was what I wanted. And I...hurt her. I nearly killed her."

I felt her sigh, the increase of pressure on my shoulders as she relaxed even deeper into me, and I couldn't help it. It was, in fact, a miracle it hadn't happened the second she touched me...my dick twitched. Pulsed with blood.

With need and desire.

For Bea.

I had to step back. Because I was going to embarrass myself.

Embarrass her.

Her arms fell off my shoulders and I was instantly cooler. My dick gave up its fight.

"But she's okay, right?" she asked, and I nodded. "Well, we'll take good care of her here and you can have twenty-four-hour visiting privileges."

I turned and walked away from the beautiful stable and the beautiful girl toward the Jeep and the other world I was trying to be happy with.

"Hey," she said, jogging to keep up with me. "Are you—"

"I'm not going to be visiting. I'll pay for her care. But I won't be here."

"Cody," she breathed, and I could tell, looking at her, that she understood. There were some things that were just too much. She reached for me again like we were going hug. Like she was going to press that bright, curvy body against mine and I put my hand up, stopping her on a dime.

"I think," I whispered. "That we've pushed our friendship as far as I can stand it today."

"Cody." She grabbed my hand and I jerked away from her, breaking the contact.

"Stop it, Bea. Jesus. I don't want your fucking pity right now."

"It's not pity."

"Whatever it is, I don't want it! I don't want you. Like that. So stop."

She jerked back, lips tight. I hadn't meant to hurt her. But if her curse was disappointing people, mine was hurting the creatures that might love me.

"I'm sorry," she whispered. "I didn't mean...to push."

And I could have said *I know*. I could have said I wanted her to touch me just as much as I was scared of it. I could have grabbed her and put that soft, tender skin of her elbows back around my neck, because that would feel so fucking good.

She...no, fuck...*we*, would feel so fucking good.

But I needed friends more than I needed to feel good.

"Let's head back," I said.

12

B EA

THIS IS a thing I know to be true. I could not, no matter how hard I might try, heal a guy's emotional wounds with my body. I could not fuck him into a better headspace. I couldn't even fuck him into liking me more than he did. Those two things were independent of each other.

Their pain.

And my spreading my legs to make it go away.

I don't want you. Like that.

I mean, that was clear as a bell. Clear as could be. Only a sucker would be thinking of going back for more. Only a sucker.

And I was the biggest sucker of all.

Was I being hard on myself? Sure. Of course. Being hard on myself was another thing I was good at. But I needed the tough love as I stood in the bright early morning light on the inside of my sliding glass door. I needed someone to stop me. To tell me to have some pride.

Ah, fuck it.

Clearly, I didn't have any. And if I wasn't going to have any, neither would he.

I opened the door. Because Cody had rejected me yesterday—well, he'd rejected my touch. And my friendship on any terms that weren't his. But I was pretty goddamned sure he'd be standing out on the other side of that tree. Watching me through the leaves and branches.

I was pretty goddamned sure he wasn't going to reject this version of me.

Stark naked, I stepped onto the deck and I dared him to try.

From the corner of my eye I caught sight of him, standing there in his old blue shirt with the tear in the collar.

When he saw me, I heard that long, slow exhale that was half moan, half laugh. The moan was for me, the laugh was at himself. I knew him enough to know that. But I didn't respond. I didn't talk to him. I didn't look his way—not that he could tell. I fed the dogs, who ate in record time and then left me alone, giving me the cold shoulder like they knew I'd gone out to the ranch without them yesterday.

And then for a few minutes I pulled the deadheads off my inpatients. Picked a ripe cherry tomato off my plant and ate it, the taste of summer bursting between my teeth. I stalled and I stalled, and the whole time I felt him there. Watching me.

If I was braver maybe I'd have said something, but I couldn't risk him recognizing my voice. The whole Miss Texas accent I'd put on when we met had faded in a big way. And frankly, it was a good thing I couldn't talk to him.

Because suddenly that was all I wanted. To put on some clothes and talk to him.

But, man, he'd made it real clear the day before that he had a limit on that kind of thing.

And maybe this version of me might get further than the real me...but I wasn't going to push my luck.

"You know," he said. "I could take three steps forward and I could probably see your face."

I stilled, gauging the three steps he needed to take and the three steps I needed to take back into my apartment.

"Or," he said, "I could sit in my truck and wait until you came out of that apartment. I mean, you have to leave sometime, right?"

I didn't answer. Because of course that was true. But... he'd never done it. Why was he talking about this? Why now?

"And I won't do those things," he said. "Because I haven't done those things. Because I'm so fucked up that this is the most straightforward relationship I have. Which makes it the best."

That stung in a stupid way. That he would prefer this to friendship was kind of a no-brainer. But still...I preferred friendship to this. I liked this plenty, but touching him yesterday, trying in my ultimately ineffective way to make him feel better—face-to-face and skin-to-skin—had changed the goddamned game for me.

The smell of his neck—sweat and sawdust and soap— was burned into my nose. I had taken such deep breaths I'd been able to taste him on the tip of my tongue. I still could.

"But let me tell you," he said. "I wish I could. I wish I could knock on your door—"

"Undo your belt," I said, even though it was stupid.

"I'm trying—"

"Undo your belt."

I wasn't looking; my back was turned to him. My eyes, instead, on my tomato plant, like I was going to use it to solve world hunger. But my ears were so finely tuned to him that I could hear the soft jangle of a buckle coming loose.

"Touch yourself," I said.

"You're not looking."

I waited for that hiss of breath that always came when he slipped his palm around the hard length of his cock. I waited...and I waited.

"I want you to look."

Fuck him, I thought.

"It doesn't mean anything if you don't look."

I laughed, deep and guttural, almost—almost like a sob. "It doesn't mean anything anyway."

And then I heard the sound of a zipper being pulled back up. That made me look.

He was doing up his belt.

"I was trying to tell you...it does mean something. To me," he said, and then—fucking nervy cowboy—he walked away.

And I stood there a long time waiting for him to come back.

But he never did.

13

CODY

I TELL YOU WHAT. I'd gotten used to the morning hand job. Even if it was me doing it. The endorphins were now expected. And without them, I was in a shit mood. And since I was in a shit mood, all I could think about was how I was screwing everything up.

Spilling my guts to my Morning Girl. Jesus. What a rookie mistake. She wasn't interested in me that way. I was feeding some kind of thrill-seeking thing with her. That's all. Some hands-off exhibitionism. Wanting more or something different was my problem.

And yesterday, giving Bea the cold shoulder after she— like a total fucking legend—dragged my ass out of trouble?

As Charlie would say, *Boy, you're an A-plus heel.*

Before noon, when I hoped Bea would be at the bar,

maybe doing some more cleaning before her shift started, I drove back into town from Gran's place. Ready to apologize.

"Hello?" I said, pushing my way through the door. It was unlocked and Chris Stapleton was playing at ear-splitting decibels, which was kind of Bea's calling card, so I had to guess she was here. "Bea?"

She came out of the kitchen with her arms full of old menus, singing maybe the saddest song ever written—"Either Way." I smiled at how painfully off-key she was. And really...really so cute with that kerchief around her head. When she saw me, she jumped and the plastic-coated menus went sliding out of her hands.

"Crap, Cody, you scared me."

"Sorry," I yelled over the music and bent to pick up the dropped menus. She smacked the menus down on the bar and turned the music off. The sudden silence pounded in my ears.

"What are you doing here?" she asked. My friendly friend from yesterday gone. Chased some chilly distance away.

"Well, we didn't finish stuff yesterday," I said.

"I got it covered."

"Bea," I said. "I'm sorry. About yesterday."

"What part?"

"What part what?"

"What part are you sorry about?" She leaned against the bar with her hip. "Because the number of men who have apologized to me because I'm mad—not because of something they did, but because I wasn't putting out anymore—is legion, Cody. Legion."

"I'm sorry I pushed you away when you were trying to be a friend. I don't...I don't have a lot of practice with friends being—"

"Friendly?"

"I was going to say pushy." I grinned at her and that tension went out of her shoulders.

"I'm not used to being a pushy friend," she said. "I'm not even all that used to being a friend."

"You're doing all right by me."

"You sure you don't want to rethink that friends with benefits thing?"

"God, yes. But how would that make anything better?"

"Oh, Cody," she sighed. "If you have to ask, you don't deserve me."

Her confidence was the hottest thing I'd seen since... well, this morning maybe.

Never in my life had I been held suspended between two women in this way. I felt, stupidly, like a web spun by two spiders. Two painfully sexy spiders.

I reached forward to pull from her dark hair some fuzz from whatever cleaning she was doing back there. Her breath left her body in a gust and I was standing close enough to her that it brushed over my parted lips and crossed my tongue.

I tasted her. The coffee she'd had. The toothpaste she'd used. Her mouth.

I got hard so fast it was almost shocking.

"Cody." It was a whisper from her mouth, another taste of her. And I wanted more. Endless more. I wanted my mouth on hers. Her tongue on mine. I wanted her body against me. I wanted to put my hands around her back. Feel the fragile span of her ribs and then...fuck, I wanted to curl my hands around her ass. I wanted to grab her ass like no one had before. Until she was moaning my name.

And every molecule of her face, of her eyes, her slack damp and pink mouth told me she wanted the same.

It would feel so good to forget for a while. To put all the shit in my head on pause so I could make this girl see some goddamned stars.

Her fingers touched my hair, too long over my ears, and her thumb brushed the thin skin of my ear lobe and it was an electric current through my whole body. It was hard to imagine what would happen if we really touched.

"We might not survive," I whispered, because we were standing close to each other now.

"What?"

"Touching each other."

"You want to find out?" Her grin was pure sass. Pure dare.

And suddenly I was thinking about the woman next door. My Morning Girl. I was thinking...about how uncomplicated it was. Until it wasn't. And I could kiss this woman, this wild, beautiful creature who turned me on and turned me inside out and it would be amazing.

Until it wasn't.

I stepped back. "I'm shit," I told her. "I really am. And as much as I want you—"

"I know."

She stroked my face and then she smacked me. Not hard. But enough that her point was made and I laughed, my skin tingling more than stinging. "And we have things we need to talk about."

"Sounds serious. We tearing apart the parking lot?"

"It's about your horse. I have—" She stood on tiptoe and reached over the bar and I looked away from the way the bottom of her shorts showed, just slightly, the sweet curve of her ass. Tender white and pink skin.

I wanted to suck that skin into my mouth. Bite it between my teeth.

God, the things I wanted to do to this woman.

"Here." She held out a couple of sheets of paper. "It's the contract for Bonnie. Just sign the bottom. You'll have all the access you want—"

"I don't want any."

"So you've said."

"This can't be right," I said, looking at the monthly amount I'd be paying. It was barely enough to cover food for her, much less the stall and the no doubt top-notch care she'd be getting.

"Friends and family discount."

"I didn't ask for that."

"I know," she said. "But I'm able to give it to you. And... it's nice. It...feels good to be on this end of things for once in my life."

"You're going to take care of transporting her, too?"

"Do you have a horse trailer?"

I laughed.

"That's what I thought. My guys will pick her up later today." She smiled at me and I smiled back. And then I just kept smiling at her. "You have to sign it, dummy," she said.

After scrawling my signature on the bottom of the contract I returned it to her and she tucked it back in her purse behind the bar and I did not—did not—stare at that skin revealed by those shorts.

"All right," she said. "That's taken care of. You here to help?"

"Depends on what you're doing."

"We have a pizza oven back there and it's literally never worked."

"And you're fixing it?"

"Moving it."

"By yourself?"

"No. You're here to help." She beamed at me and in that minute I would have done anything she asked. Anything.

BEA

OVER THE SOUND of the shower I heard my phone ringing, and I had high hopes that it would be my sister so I jumped out of the shower, slid hard on the tiles, and banged my hip on the towel rack.

I yanked on the towel, wrapping it around my body as I ran into the TV room where my phone was plugged in.

"Ronnie?" I cried.

"No. Sorry. Bea, it's Oscar."

"Oscar! What's going on?" I sat down on the edge of my couch and Thelma approached to lick the water drops off my knee.

"They won't let us leave with the horse."

"Bonnie? Why?"

"Because the owner has to sign off."

"Cody didn't sign off?"

"He's not listed as the owner. A guy named Charlie Hoynes is the owner."

Charlie... I remembered Cody mentioning a Charlie. But not that he owned Bonnie. This didn't make sense.

"Do they have his number?"

"Yeah. They gave it to me. I left a message... but—"

"Oscar. I'm so sorry. I didn't realize there would be a hiccup like this. Text me the number and go on home. I'll take care of this."

"Okay. No problem. I'll send the number once we hang up."

We hung up and I rubbed Thelma between her eyes in that place she liked and waited for my phone to buzz with the text from Oscar.

And then I looked down at the phone number in my texts and wondered what was the right thing to do. Call Cody. Call this Charlie guy.

I didn't have Cody's phone number so the solution was simple. But it didn't feel that way. It felt very complicated.

As Cody's friend I imagined he'd want me to call Charlie. Because he didn't want to deal with the horse he'd hurt. But as Cody's friend that felt like a betrayal.

But as Bea King—I was really, really curious. And I didn't have a choice.

I pressed the button and called this Charlie guy.

"Yello?" he answered on the third ring.

"Charlie Hoynes?" I asked and stood up, tucking the towel a little tighter around my chest. Like he could see me.

"Speaking. Who's this?"

"My name is Bea King—"

"King? You related to Hank?"

"He was my father."

"Well, girl, you have my condolences."

"I take it you knew my father?" I laughed.

"Did a few deals with him until I learned my lesson," he said. "What can I do for you, Bea?"

"Well, I'm friends with Cody McBride."

"Again. You have my condolences."

"That's not funny," I said, fast and angry.

"If you're not laughing now, trust me you will. That boy got broke and no one bothered to fix him."

I can.

The thought burbled up from that part of my brain I tried to ignore. The part of my brain where all my worst ideas came from. The part of my brain that gave me black eyes and broken hearts more times than not.

That part of my brain was ready to suit up and try to fix Cody. When I knew, knew in every other part of my body, that it was a bad idea.

"Well, I'm calling because the farm where Cody put Bonnie after the accident has you down as the owner."

"Yep," he said.

"And I'm transferring Bonnie to my farm—"

"King's Land? That's rich."

"Literally," I said a little stiffly. "But without your consent, I can't move Bonnie."

"Does Cody know you're doing this?"

"He signed a contract with me."

Charlie sighed, heavy and long. Like he was just so damn tired.

"No," he said.

"What?"

"I'm not signing the paperwork."

"Charlie, whatever beef you had with my dad, let me assure you—"

"Bea. It's not your father. It's not Bonnie going to King's Land. It's entirely about Cody getting other people to do the hard work, just like he always has."

"Nothing about this is hard," I said. "I just need to be able to move Bonnie—"

"It's not hard for you. And frankly, sweetheart, it's not hard for me. It's hard for him. It's hard for him to look at that horse. And to talk to me. And my guess is he hasn't told you much about his mother."

"Charlie!" I snapped. "That's not—"

"Has he? Talked about his mother? His grandmother?"

"Yes. He has."

"That she liked fancy drinks and smoked menthol Virginia Slims and maybe that she was a stewardess?"

"Yes," I said. "He told me that."

"He hasn't told you shit."

I bristled right up and I imagined if I was face-to-face with this guy I'd have my hand in a fist and I'd be thinking about a well-placed throat punch.

"The horse needs to be dealt with," I said. "The doctors say she's better."

"And I've dealt with it. She's paid up for another month. When he wants to move Bonnie, he's got to call me. He's got to talk to me."

"Just to be clear, you're holding that horse hostage."

"I guess you could say that."

"I don't know if I like you, Charlie."

"Cody always said the same thing. But when things went to shit I was the only friend he had left standing. So he owes me."

I hung up the phone and pulled off my towel, dropping it on Thelma's head. She barked and ran around until it fell off. I got dressed and went downstairs, hoping Jack would be down there. And would be willing to give me Cody's number.

14

I pushed open the door to the bar only to find Jack sitting poring over the designs for the expansion. He had a tumbler full of booze with about seven cherries at the bottom of it. My watch said it was three in the afternoon. A little early for all those cherries.

None of that boded well.

"Jack," I said. The bar was dim but clean and it smelled better than it had in days, thanks to all my hard work and the clean, fresh smell of sawdust. The plastic sheeting between the bar and the relatively open space next door billowed in the breeze.

There were a few customers around and Kimmy at the bar had things in hand.

"Bea," he said. "What are you doing here?"

"Well, I need you to break some employee/employer confidentiality."

"Great. I was in the mood for that."

"I need Cody's number."

He looked up at me through the dark hair that flopped over his eyes. "Don't, Bea."

"Don't what?"

"Do...what you do."

That stung. I looked away so he wouldn't see the pain I wasn't sure I could hide.

"Bea," he whispered. "It's not like that."

"It's not like what? Not like you're worried I'll hurt your friend? Fuck him and leave him? Break his heart?"

"I'm worried he'll break yours just as much as you'll break his," he said quietly. "You're the two most self-destructive people I know and I'm worried you'll go running right into that mess."

Because I liked messes. Messes were my happy place. And if it wasn't messy, I'd make shit messy, just so I felt comfortable. This thing I was doing, stripping for him in the morning and being friends with him in the afternoon—it was a mess. Because I was making it that way. Another kind of woman, another kind of friend, wouldn't do that.

"I don't think he's a mess," I said.

"You don't know him."

"I know him plenty!" I cried, wondering why all of a sudden there was a hierarchy to friendship with this guy. Everyone out to prove they knew more than me. I doubt Jack ever spread his legs for Cody.

"How am I friends with him?" Jack asked, swiveling on his stool.

"You like lost causes?"

"I'm assuming that's some kind of crack about me trusting you and wanting you to manage the bar."

I shrugged, hummed in my throat, and he laughed at me. "We were talking about you. And Cody."

"Summer camp," he said.

"You're joking."

He shook his head, smiling as if the memories were just

so sweet. "Well, that's what they called it. But it was kind of a rehab program for kids in trouble."

"Drugs trouble?"

"All kinds," he said. "Cody showed up with a black eye and a broken hand. Took a swing at me, like, five minutes after we met."

That kind of anger made sense. It was there in Cody, behind his shyness. Behind his rules and distance. There was a sense of something burning there, just behind his blue eyes. Under his freckled skin.

That's what Jack was telling me. That's why I needed to be careful. But I had my own anger just under my skin.

"Why were you there?" I asked.

Jack sighed heavily out his nose and picked up his glass, only to find it empty except for cherries. "You don't have to answer if you don't want."

"I was seventeen, my girlfriend was sixteen and her father caught us having sex. Had me arrested."

"Oh my God."

"Could have been worse."

"How?"

"Well, I could have gotten out of that camp and turned right around and married her."

I laughed. "Yeah. That would make things worse."

If we had that kind of relationship, I'd hug him. But he was still my boss. And Jack was not a hugger.

"I appreciate the information, about Cody," I said. "And the insight. But I need Cody's number so we can deal with his horse. I'm taking his horse to our stables. And there's a hiccup in the paperwork."

He fished out his phone and soon mine buzzed. "There," he said. "But I'm telling you it won't do you any good. He never has it on him. You're better off just going out to his house."

A seedy thrill raced through me. The idea of seeing Cody in his natural state was an exciting one. Risky. What might happen if we weren't at the bar, surrounded by my lies and his obligations?

"I don't know where he lives."

"You remember Edna McBride's house on Elm?" I nodded. Edna's house was a local legend. "If you go out there, take the guy some food. He's half feral." Jack sat back down, looked at the blueprint, and picked up his glass, swearing when he found it empty again.

"Can I make you a drink?"

"Please, god," he said, and I stepped behind the bar over the plastic sheeting. Since the place was open, some of the bottles and glasses had been restocked on the bar.

He'd made what looked like Bourbon Sours without the sour mix and only bourbon and cherry juice. The ice machine was working because I'd cleaned out the lines and I scooped some into my shaker, which I'd polished up to a high shine.

"What's got you so worked up?" I asked him. "About those plans."

"What am I doing?" he breathed. "Like...what do I actually think I'm doing?"

"Making a very successful bar more successful."

"It feels like I'm just taking a dive bar and making it bigger."

"Jack—"

"I don't have the money for all the things you're about to say. The guy who can cook. The kitchen he can cook in. A fucking pizza oven. That bar thing you and Cody talked about—"

"I can loan you the money."

He blinked at me and I blinked back.

Did I say that out loud?

"*You* want to loan me money?"

I guess I did. I'd said it and now it was out there.

"Bea," he said, shaking his head into my silence. "You don't have to—"

"I want to." It was true. I could feel it in my body. That strange sensation of being right. And doing the right thing. It was the same as when I offered a stall to Bonnie. The same as when I took my sister out of that room when Clayton was shredding her heart to pieces. I didn't know this feeling that well, that sharp burst of it in my chest.

Pride and a kind of glee.

A deep, warm happiness.

Yeah, I could get used to this.

"I do."

"Bea, there's a good chance I'm a bad bet."

"Nah. I know bad bets. You are not a bad bet."

"Do you come with the loan?"

I scowled at him. "All this time and you never hit on me and you're hitting on me now?"

"You as a manager."

"Oh." I gave myself what was left of the drink I'd poured him in a small tumbler. For courage.

"I'd bet on you. Every day of the week." His quiet voice sent shivers down my spine. What was I doing with so many friends? I wondered. How did this happen? My sister leaves for New York and I just branch off on my own. She was going to come back and I wasn't going to be a mess for her to solve. Or a problem.

What would we talk about?

Oh, right, going back to school.

"That's nice," I said, which was such an understatement I couldn't stand it. "But the loan comes with some paperwork and I'll keep cleaning the place out. But I'm no one's boss. How much do you think you'll need?"

"Ten grand?"

"Are you just trying to be cheap, or do you really not know?"

"If I buy used equipment and just tell the cook to watch a few more episodes of Iron Chef?" He was only joking about part of that.

"You're not buying used equipment. Not with my money. Let me see those plans."

We decided on twenty-five grand and I talked him down from seven percent interest to five.

I lifted my glass. "To making the biggest and best dive bar in Texas."

"Let's do it," he said. And we shot back our drinks.

"I gotta go deal with this Cody thing," I said.

"Yeah, good luck."

"I'll talk to the bank and we can meet tomorrow."

"Tomorrow."

I grabbed my purse and headed back outside onto the quiet main street of Dusty Creek. There wasn't a lot of stuff going on in this town. Patsy's Pies across the street had been there since the dawn of time. The auto-parts store kept changing owners, but never seemed to go under. Bishops. The Hexagon Hotel. The Farm and Fleet up the way was a new build and a popular one. The Piggly Wiggly. The jewelry store that mostly just replaced watch batteries, and the florist where the boys bought girls corsages for homecoming. There was a Casey's out by the highway. But that was pretty much it for businesses along the main drag.

Except...right across the street was Sabrina's new bakery.

She'd been open two months and I hadn't gone in except for the grand opening.

She'd managed to rope Ronnie and me into walking around with trays of her cupcakes and tarts. Those little meringues that were—I could safely say because she wasn't here to hear me say it—the best things I'd ever eaten in my life.

Except for that Saturday afternoon two months ago, I hadn't even looked in the window. Every time I'd seen her, she was bringing me coffee beside the ravine.

The bakery had a pink-and-white awning with Sweet Things printed in a classy script. Without a doubt it was the most elegant thing in Dusty Creek. By a mile. And it was lined up out the door most mornings, which I felt said the people of Dusty Creek were ready for something different.

Jack could be a little different. There was room there for him to try.

And Sabrina could help me figure some business stuff out.

Though I knew how that conversation would go.

She'd make fun of me for giving my money to Jack. She would talk me out of it; my sister had always had that knack. To talk me back down to size.

Shove me back in the box of my mistakes.

Of course, she only did it to me because I did it to her first.

Tomorrow, maybe. I'd make an effort to go over and see her. Be nice. See how the shop was doing. *Maybe Jack could serve her desserts in the bar.*

The idea was an excellent one and would be great for everyone. Tomorrow, I decided, and pulled out my phone and entered Cody's number.

It rang about seven hundred times and finally went to

voice mail. A robotic voice told me to leave a message, which I didn't bother to do. Instead, I walked back to my Jeep and headed out to Elm Avenue with a quick stop at Buddy's on the south side for brisket and mac and cheese. And then I grabbed a six of Shiner at Casey's because brisket without Shiner was un-American.

And...I won't lie. I figured a couple of drinks between us might...I don't know. Loosen things up. Change the dynamic. Make him forget his rules.

Make me forget what a mistake touching him might be.

It'd been many years since I was last at Edna's house, and as I drove slowly down Elm I realized that all I really remembered about it were her amazing garden and...yep... there it was. The bright green door.

Faded a little, but still there.

Bright green with a big gold lion-head knocker right smack dab in the middle of it.

The garden out front was a wild mess of dried-out brambles and overgrown plants. I didn't blame Cody for not taking care of it, because of his bad knee but it didn't change the fact that Enid would be so sad to see her garden that way.

I hoped, I really did, that I wasn't making a mistake.

Ah, hell, who was I kidding? Mistakes were what I excelled at. I grabbed the BBQ, went up to that bright green door, and prepared myself to make a doozy of one.

15

C ODY

CHARLIE WAS CALLING ME. A lot. So I put my phone in my underwear drawer and did my physical therapy in the living room. Where I couldn't hear it.

I did the therapy on the ball and with the sissy little bands and the five-pound ankle weights until I was drenched in sweat. Until every muscle shook and it felt like half my brain had shut down.

Never in my life had I expected my ass to be so thoroughly kicked by physical therapy. At the top of my game I could run a six-minute mile and bench double my weight. I had belt buckles that proved I was a badass.

Now I was getting that bad ass kicked by the stretchy bands.

In the bedroom I took off my sweat-soaked shirt and tossed it in the vicinity of my hamper. I took out fresh clothes, and because it was there and I had limited self-control...I fished out my phone.

Four calls from an unknown number. Another bunch from Charlie and three text messages. And, I swear to god, I wasn't going to read those texts but I caught sight of Bea's name.

She seems like a nice girl and she's already falling for you.

What the fuck? Why was Charlie talking to Bea? And falling for me? Where in the world did he get that idea?

And just like that, my phone buzzed and Charlie's number appeared and all my avoiding him went up in smoke. All the really good reasons I had for not returning his phone calls were not nearly as important as finding out what he was doing talking to Bea.

"Charlie?"

"'Bout damn time, boy."

That *boy* grated. The *boy* always grated, and he knew it and it was why he was calling me that. But his voice...god. His voice. The whiskey-soaked baritone of it, just this side of a rasp.

I think you got talent. Real talent, boy. I remembered that. *But you're wasting it.* And I remembered that.

"What are you doing?" I asked him, getting to the point. Because once the memories came back I was never going to make my way clear of them again.

"Son—"

"Don't, Charlie. Don't." If there was one thing I hated more than *boy* it was *son*. *Son* said in that particular tone. In that particular way. Because he had been a father to me. And that hadn't worked out very well for either of us. "What bug is up your ass?"

His silence was awful, so awful I wanted to hang up. I remembered all at once exactly why I hadn't talked to him in months. Because we had so much to say. None of it good. None of it easy.

"You want to move Bonnie," he said.

"How'd you know?"

"Because when I moved her there after the accident, I said I was the owner. Because you didn't have a phone. And were in and out of surgery."

I pinched the bridge of my nose. "I...know. You don't have to explain it to me."

"So, you need my okay to move her."

"So, give it."

"Nope."

"What do you want Charlie?"

"Meet me there. At the rehab place."

"Charlie—"

"Meet me there, son. And look me in the eye and tell me why you haven't returned my calls. Meet me there and talk to me."

The *no* was on the tip of my tongue. The *no* was pushing its way out of my mouth. Into the world.

"I deserve that, Cody. And you know it. And maybe you do, too."

"I got what I deserved," I said with a laugh.

"I talked to Bea," he said, twisting the screws. "She seems like a firecracker. The kind of girl you used to like. The kind that would be good—"

"Tomorrow," I said. "Noon. At the rehab place."

"Looking forward to it, son."

"Don't," I whispered, "call me son."

But he'd already hung up. I looked down at my phone and felt the power in my muscles to heave it against the wall. To drop it and crush it under my heel. But there was a loud knocking on my door and so all I did was toss the phone back in my underwear drawer and limp my way to the front hall.

It could only be Jack, so I didn't bother with a shirt. It could only be Jack, so I didn't bother trying to check my temper and bad attitude.

"Don't you have anything better to do?" I demanded as I threw open the door.

"Nope," Bea answered.

She had a take-out container filled with what smelled like Buddy's brisket in one hand and a six-pack of Shiner in the other. And everything in between those two things lit me on fire. The bright red lips, the deep V-neck of her blue T-shirt, the long skirt that ran over her hips and thighs like water.

Her sparkling eyes and the razor-sharp edge of her smile.

I was tired of fighting her. Of fighting...this. And all the anger and grief and guilt I was feeling seemed to reach out for her. Seemed to want her.

She will make me feel better, my body seemed to say. *She is what I want.*

"What are you doing here?"

"I thought we could have a few beers. Talk—"

"That's a bad idea."

"The beers or the talking?"

"All of it. Everything. You," I snapped at her, "are a bad idea."

She winced and glanced away. I'd hurt her. And I felt like shit about it, but this was a her-or-me situation. This was fight or flight. And I'd run from her as far as I could. My back was against the wall and she just kept on coming.

"Funny," she said with a cracked voice and brave smile that took me out at the knees. "I think I've heard that somewhere before. Here." She shoved the Shiner and the takeout container at me, and I took them because I didn't know what else to do. "You've got some shit to figure out with your horse," she said, backing away.

"Bea," I said, feeling as if my guts were stuck on the bottom of her shoe. She was pulling part of me with her, every step she took. "Bea, wait—"

She turned and lifted her middle finger at me over her shoulder. And I deserved that and so much more, but she didn't deserve what I'd done to her. I dropped the stuff in my arms beside the door and ran after her.

I caught her at the curb beside her Jeep. "Bea," I said. "I'm sorry. I really am."

"Yeah, fuck you." She didn't look at me but I could see the tears swimming in the corners of her eyes.

"No, listen—"

"No, you listen." She shoved me away from her but I wouldn't go. I wasn't rock solid on my feet, but I was rock solid with this. With her. "You don't get to say that to me. No one does anymore. You know why? Because I'm not a bad idea. I'm not."

"Bea—"

"Don't!"

I grabbed her forearm. Well, not so much grabbed as touched, and we both sucked in a breath. Hers was probably furious. But mine was...fuck...mine was rattled and turned inside out.

How many times had we touched? There was that hug the other day. The handshake a few days ago. I'd never really touched her like this. The whole of my palm touching some part of her body, some sweet stretch of her skin.

"Stop touching me," she said.

I wasn't holding her, she could literally just move her arm. So could I. But we didn't.

"I don't want to stop," I said.

"What about your rules?" she asked. "What about dragging me down with you?"

My fingers twitched and stroked that sensitive pale skin on the inside of her arm. I could, in fact, feel the pound of her heart in her wrist. She was panting and so was I, our breathing matched like we were in this race together.

Don't look at her, I told myself, even as my hand sought new territory of her body to touch. I cupped her elbow, my fingers easing up under the sleeve of her shirt. She was sweating, which I loved. Because so was I.

And she was shaking. Trembling.

So was I.

"Cody," she said, and then I did it. I looked at her. And I fell headfirst into her wide blue gaze.

This was a mistake. Touching her like this. Wanting her like this. No good would come of it. I should stick to my Morning Girl. The perfect simplicity of it. No one got hurt with my Morning Girl. No one.

This—me and Bea—we'd both get hurt.

"I don't care," I said.

"Yeah. Me neither," she said, and then I wasn't just touching her. I grabbed her arm and turned her, putting her back to her Jeep. And I stepped right into her. Right up against her. My cock, painfully hard, pressed against her belly and we both sighed.

"You want this," I said, grinding just a little against her because it felt so good. Because her eyes were blown wide. Because I couldn't help myself.

"Yes," she said.

I braced my arms against the Jeep, squeezing the metal frame until my palms hurt.

Don't let go, I told myself.

And then I kissed her. My mouth to the lemon-sweet spice of hers. And she opened right away, like she was gasping she opened her mouth and her arms came around my back, holding me so hard.

Yes. Fuck, yes. There was nothing careful. Nothing easy or tentative. We kissed like we knew each other and had been separated for far too long.

Her hips arched forward, pressing my cock between our bodies, and I groaned low in my throat. Taking her mouth with no finesse. Nothing but hunger. And she met me the same way. I sucked on her tongue and her fingers pulled my hair and I could have died, right there, a happy man. Such a happy man.

Because she tasted perfect. Felt perfect. Like home.

Like something I missed and hadn't realized how much.

I eased back, suddenly scared. Suddenly in way too deep.

"Don't you dare," she said and followed me. This time it was her sucking my tongue and I groaned, falling back against her and the Jeep. And, again, my cock hit her just right and she arched up against me, bracing her feet against the curb until she found the spot she wanted and I felt her tension. The electric current filling her body.

And fuck, I was going to see where that current went. I was going to follow it all the way to the end. But for that we needed to not be standing on the street in front of all my neighbors.

I let go of the Jeep's metal frame and cupped her shoulders, the raw, fierce strength of her arms, until finally I had her hand in mine and I stepped back.

She stumbled forward, her eyes blissed out, her lips swollen. And fuck, the things I wanted to do to her. The shit I wanted to say. I wanted to crank every dial she had until it was way past bearable. Until she was screaming my name and coming so hard it hurt.

"Inside," I said, and I turned, my cock bouncing as I walked, pushed so obscenely against the fabric of my gym shorts. If anyone was paying attention I know I looked ridiculous.

And I did not give one shit.

Her hand in mine, I practically ran up the walk to my house and we were barely through my open front door before I turned and pushed her up against the wall, slamming the front door shut with my foot.

"Holy shit," she said. "Look at this place—"

"Later," I said and crowded right up into her. I braced my arms against the wall and kissed her again. Kissed her until she was pushing back against me. Kissed her until she was grinding herself against my cock.

Behind my closed eyelids I saw stars.

She pulled back and I followed, but her hand against my chest stopped me.

"Are you going to touch me?" she asked, whispered, really, against my lips.

And I didn't know how to tell her that in so many ways I was scared to. I was barely on the edge of something wild, and touching her fucking body would send me someplace I couldn't contain.

"Cody," she breathed into my silence, and then her hands lifted to my shoulders, still wet with sweat, and then skated down over my biceps and onto my chest. Her fingers touched my nipples, grazed them until I groaned and then she came back for more. She stroked my abs, first with the palm of her hand and then with the back of her hand, and I watched her watching me. And when her fingertips reached the waistband of my shorts I nearly came.

I grabbed her hands, pushing them back against her body.

She pushed against me, but she didn't stand a chance.

"Touch me and I'll come, Bea." I shook my head. "I'm barely—"

"Me, too."

I looked in her eyes. Looked at her face, the high flush and the way she was gulping air. I could see her heart pounding in the tender skin of her throat.

"Cody," she breathed, her back bowing off the wall and into my sweat-slick chest. "Please. I've wanted you..."

"For so long," I finished her sentence. Even if that wasn't what she meant, it was how I felt. Like I'd wanted her for eons, not just days. Years. Not hours.

But still I was a powder keg and everything about me felt dangerous. I turned her around so she faced the wall. The sweet curve of her ass pressed up against my dick and I hissed between my teeth at the contact.

She tried to turn back around but I wouldn't let her. My fingers threaded through hers and that contact, the soft webbing of our palms touching, was like fire under my skin. I pushed her palms up against the wall.

"Keep them there," I said and dropped my hands to her hips.

"Cody." She reached for me and I stepped back. Away from her, the sudden air between us felt arctic. My skin without hers touching it felt like ice.

"Don't..." Fuck, it sounded stupid. Over-dramatic, but I was barely holding on here. "...touch me."

16

She stood against the wall. So still. "Is this another one of your rules?" she whispered.

"Rules?"

Did I have rules with Bea? Other than not doing this? Other than avoiding this at all costs?

She bowed her head against the wall. "Never mind... just...do what you're going to do."

She lifted her hands up wider against the wall, and the muscles under her shirt shifted and bunched. Her sleeves pulled back to show her shoulders, the sweet indention of her muscles. I wanted to kiss her there, but there was no time.

Her fingers spread wide against Gran's old wallpaper and the position made her hips pop out from the wall.

What I was going to do made my mouth water. My hands cupped her waist and slid down to her hips;, my thumb brushed the curve of her ass and she twisted a little under my touch all the muscles firing under my palms.

I liked that.

My thumbs slipped down over the curve of her ass to that sweet crease where her thigh started.

I thought again of my Morning Girl, of how badly I'd wanted to touch her the other day. How hard it had been not to climb to that deck. With her I had rules. So many rules.

"Cody," she breathed, and I realized I was stroking that sweat tender skin through the stretchy thin fabric of her skirt. She put her forehead against the wall and made some whimpering sound in the back of her throat like I was just killing her.

"You okay?" I asked.

"Please," she whispered, and her begging went right to my head like a shot of whiskey.

With both hands I pulled up that skirt, revealing bit by bit the long lengths of her legs.

And then the red panties she wore beneath it. They were sliding down her hips and I wanted them on the floor. I wanted them in my pocket.

"Hold your skirt," I whispered in her ear, and her hands came off the wall to grab the gathered skirt out of my grasp. With my hands free I slipped them down over the silk of her panties, over her ass and then around...slowly...so slowly...to her pussy.

"Fuck," I breathed when I found her ready. Drenched and hot. She was soaked, her panties were soaked, the insides of her thighs were soaked. "You're so wet, Bea."

"I want you. So bad," she groaned.

Teasing her, teasing both of us, I played with the lace trim on the top of her panties, running my fingers over it until she whimpered and her legs sagged.

"I like it when you beg me," I whispered.

"Oh, my god, please, Cody. Please."

"What?"

"Touch me."

"Like this?" I slipped my fingers down another inch into her panties. I could feel the heat coming from her. The tickle of her pubic hair against my fingers.

"No, asshole," she groaned and grabbed my hand, shoving it deep into her underwear until I was cupping the whole of her pussy in the palm of my hand. My fingers slipped right through the fat, wet lips and found the entrance to her body. I rimmed her with my fingers. Light touches, around and around until her hips were following the movements. And I pushed my heel down until I found the pressure and the place that made her stand up on her tiptoes.

"How bad do you want it?" I asked her.

"Cody," she moaned, her head back against my shoulder, and I put my lips to her throat.

"Tell me, Bea."

"I feel like I'm dying," she whispered. "I'm so empty inside it hurts. I need you—"

I slid my middle finger deep into her body and she cried out. Her knees buckling, she turned her head against my shoulder and I knew she wanted me to kiss her. But I was in danger of burning up right there on the spot. I was about to be a giant pile of ash.

We both fell against the wall. The heel of my hand pressed harder against her clit and she started to shake.

Rules. A little self-control. Restraint.

"Stop," I said.

"I can't, I can't. Cody. I'm so close...so close—"

I pulled my hands away from her body, because I wanted my mouth on her when she did it. I wanted to taste her. Feel her.

"No!" she cried out. "What are you doing?"

I stepped back and she turned, dropping her skirt. She leaned back against the wall. Her eyes so blissed out, her skin pink and red. Her nipples against that shirt.

Jesus, god.

I looked up at the ceiling and prayed for strength.

"You want to watch me do it?" she whispered. She began lifting her skirt. "Is that your thing?"

My body tautened.

"Does that help you keep all your rules intact? Does that help you keep things from getting messy? You don't mind the come, it's the feelings you don't want all over your hands."

Fuck. She nailed it. That was the whole appeal of My Morning Girl. Well, clearly not all of the appeal.

Why was I thinking about her right now? Why were they so confused in my head?

Bea bunched that skirt up around her waist and tucked it behind her back so her hands were free. And her hands went down to the soaking red silk of her underwear, pulled askew by my hands.

"It won't feel as good without you," she whispered. Her eyes were losing that blissed-out look, and instead her gaze was sharpening its way into a blade and her mouth wasn't soft and kissable anymore. It was a straight line. "The one time I'm going to let you touch me and you don't want a piece of this?"

"One time?"

"Your rules are a drag, Cody. I don't fuck guys with so many rules."

I shoved her up against that wall, my body flat against hers. She gasped, but her eyes on mine did not lose their edge. And her anger made the air taste like smoke.

"I like you like this," I told her, looking down into that pissed-off sweetheart of a face of hers.

"I don't like you much at all."

I didn't call her a liar, but I bent my knees and arced my cock up against the heat and wet of her. And I did it again and again. Until her lips parted on a moan and the skin of her neck went red.

"You want to know why I stopped?"

"Because you're a coward?"

Yes. But that was a different conversation. "Because I want to taste you as you come. I want all of this..." My hand slid down over her wet pussy. "All over my mouth. Because I want to suck on your clit until you scream my fucking name. Because my fingers inside of you isn't enough, I want it to be my tongue—"

"Then do it," she spat.

Oh, man, how easy it would be to love this woman. Maybe I already did. I couldn't unravel the threads of what I felt.

Her face softened. "Do it," she whispered. "Please."

And I got down in front of her as best I could, I found a position my knee could live with for the moment, knowing I would pay for this later. But now, right now, I was drunk on her. Drunk on the smell of her, the heat I could feel on my face. I put my mouth right over the wettest part of those panties and she flinched against me like I'd touched her with fire.

God, the taste of her. I'd go to bed tonight and probably every other night for months thinking about this, right here. The salty sweetness of this woman's pussy. I sucked on her until she cried out. Until her knees buckled again.

And then I got serious.

I pulled that underwear out of the way, leaving it just

above her knees because I liked the way that looked. Dirty and desperate.

My cock was so hard it hurt. But like I did with anything I couldn't be bothered to feel while I was competing, I put it out of my head. My body was down the list of shit that mattered.

She was so primed I could feel the tension in her body.

"You're so ready, Bea," I whispered, blowing against her pussy. I saw goose bumps lift against the skin of her thighs.

"Hurry."

I laughed. No fucking way was I hurrying. This might be my only time on my knees in front of this woman. I wasn't going to waste my shot. With my thumbs I stroked the edges of those lips, pulling them back just slightly until I saw the pink of her and then...there. the glossy hard ridge of her clit.

"Look at you. So pink. So pretty."

She made some indecipherable groaning sound in her throat. She was getting pissed but was too far gone to push me away.

"I like you like this," I said and pressed a kiss against that clit and then pulled away. She followed me with her hips, but I pushed her back against the wall. "So fucking desperate to come you don't even care that you're mad at me. I can play with you all day and you'd let me."

"Don't you fucking dare," she said.

From my position on my knees I looked up at her. "You're beautiful," I told her.

"Make me come."

I laughed in my throat. My belly. My fucking heart. And I did what she asked.

I put my mouth right to that pretty clit and sucked and a slid a finger deep inside her and I could tell it wasn't enough, so I gave her another one and I found that fleshy spot inside her body and I gave it some love, too.

And, god, there would be nothing in my life as amazing as this woman coming against my mouth. Her come ran down my hand and the walls of her pussy clenched down hard on my fingers.

Her fingers gripped my head, pushing me into her, holding me there until all I could breathe was her scent. She shook and she shook and she cried out high and loud, and when she finally stopped she slid down the wall until she was sitting across my knees.

"Oh, my god," she whispered. Her hands were over her face, her skirt draped over us like a blanket. I could feel the heat of her pussy through my shorts.

"You okay?" I whispered and pulled her hand away from her face. "No, baby," I breathed, horror flooding my body so hard and so fast I nearly gagged. Because she was crying. Tears clung to her lower eyelashes. "I hurt you."

When would I learn? When would I fucking learn? It didn't matter what my intentions were, I hurt everything I touched. I struggled to get to my feet, but my knee made it impossible, and instead I ended up bracing my arm against the wall and trying to use it for leverage to stand up.

She stopped me by putting her hand on my cock. The heat of her palm made the fabric of my shorts irrelevant. Her touched seared me. Scorched me.

"I'm crying because you made me feel so good," she said.

That was some Grade A bullshit and I shook my head.

"It's true, Cody."

"I have to—" I said and then stopped because my weakness was suddenly too much. "My knee, Bea."

She let go of me and actually helped me to my feet. The

embarrassment was chilling. I couldn't look at her. I couldn't fucking stand it.

"Are you okay?" she asked.

No. "Fine."

"I'm sorry," she said. She was on her feet, too, between me and the wall. Her breasts, when she took that deep inhale, touched my chest and I stepped away.

"Yeah." My laugh was dry and awful. Because inside I was dry and awful. "Me too."

"Don't..." She cupped my face in her hands and I wanted to shrug her off. I wanted to step away but I was in so much pain and her touch felt so damn good. "You don't mean that."

"Don't I?"

"You're not sorry you touched me. And I'm not sorry I let you. That was the best orgasm of my life, Cody."

I pulled my face away because there was something similar about her words. About the tone.

You'll get back on your feet. You'll be better before you know it.

I stepped back and my knee lurched, and she reached forward to grab me but I pushed her hands away.

"Cody," she said, still coming for me.

"This is over."

She blinked at me and I sounded like a dick. I got that a hundred percent, but I needed her to go. I was in pieces here.

"Look at you," she said. And I knew what she was looking at. I was a fucking mess. I'd nearly come about 800 times in my shorts and I was hard as stone and probably would be for days. "Please. Let me touch you—"

Watching her face so I could see exactly what kind of pain I caused, I slipped my hand into my shorts. I bit my lip against the pleasure that was so sharp it was practically painful.

"Don't," she whispered.

Yeah. I did it anyway. Three hard strokes and my orgasm exploded through me. I forced myself not to shut my eyes. Not to stagger back. I stood, rock solid, and watched her face go white and distant.

I pulled my hand out and wiped it off on the back of my shorts, and finally she looked away. She hiked up her skirt as if to show me everything I'd had in my grasp and never would again but it was really only so she could pull up her underwear.

Her legs were splayed out differently than they had been when I was between them, or maybe I was just less distracted, but I caught a glimpse of what looked like a birthmark, on the inside of her thigh.

My Morning Girl had the same mark.

But then she dropped her skirt and I told myself it was a shadow and a trick of my mind. It had to be, right? I couldn't even process it so I did what I did with everything I couldn't process.

I shoved it aside to be dealt with later.

She grabbed her purse from where it had fallen on the other side of the door, next to the brisket and the beer. When she stood she put her hands through her hair and sighed heavily, the kind of sigh that, if she were alone, maybe would be a scream.

"This," I said, my voice a sandpaper rasp. "Is why I had the rules."

"I don't give a shit."

"I don't want to hurt anyone anymore," I told her. As plain as I could. My soul right there.

That made her look at me and I couldn't read her

expression. Her face could have been carved from marble. And not for the first time and probably not for the last I thought—*Jesus. She's so damn pretty.*

I could tell she wanted to say something. She probably had a laundry list of shit she wanted to say. About how I hurt her anyway. About how I was hurting myself more than I was hurting anyone else. All of it completely true. But it didn't change anything. And maybe she figured that out, because she grabbed her purse, opened the door.

And walked away.

And I spent my night drinking that Shiner.

Thinking about birthmarks and lies.

17

B EA

THAT WAS...WELL, that was a lot of things. But mostly it was what I deserved.

It was a miracle I got into my Jeep, my hands were shaking so hard. When I sat, I winced because he'd used my clit hard. Tears burned behind my eyes again.

Don't, I told myself. *Don't sit in front of his house and cry. Don't be that girl.*

I started the Jeep and turned the corner around the block and tried not to do it. Tried with every foot between me and that broken-down, emotionally stunted cowboy to shore myself up. To get my armor back in place.

But it didn't work. I pulled over and stared out the windshield at the Dusty Creek Elementary playground, empty except for a mother with a stroller and a toddler she was pushing on a swing.

You'll be okay, I told myself. It was the first in a long litany of things I used to tell myself when I was a kid. When my dad or stepmom would say some shitty thing about me.

They don't know you. Not really.

That's how bad Cody had just hurt me. H'de knocked me right back into my childhood.

Somehow, someway, I'd given him access to that little spot in me. That core place that no one saw. No one got to know. Because he did fucking know me.

The tears came hard. Like sobs. And I gave myself three of them. And then I pushed the tears off my face. Hardened the soft, miserable parts of myself that he'd bruised. What hurt the most, maybe, was how intentionally he'd done it. How clear he'd made it that every second against that wall was a mistake for him.

A regret.

I'd been a lot of men's mistake. And I'd regretted a lot of men.

But Cody...fuck. Cody was different. Or I'd thought he was, anyway. Stupid me. Again. How many men had I thought were different only to have them treat me the same as every other man?

But even as I thought that it seemed wrong. Cody had hurt me. A slice right through the heart. But not like the other men who'd hurt me, because they'd been lying all the time and Cody...Cody never once lied.

It was me, always me, that was lying to him.

A couple of deep breaths and I had myself back under control. This was for the best. I had been in danger of falling for that guy. And falling pretty hard. It wasn't nice what he did, but it was the reminder I needed.

Cody was not for me.

· · ·

WHEN I GOT BACK to my apartment, I parked behind Sweet Things because Sabrina had two parking spots back there and she only used the one. Which saved me from having to buy a parking permit for the street.

We usually never saw each other. Her hours were different from mine and I tried pretty damn hard not to run into her. But tonight the lights were on in the bakery and the air smelled like buttery crust in the oven.

And I wanted my sister. But Ronnie was on the other side of the continent and Sabrina was the only sister option open to me.

She probably won't make you feel better, I told myself. Because we weren't those kinds of sisters.

But we were some kind of sisters and I was desperate.

The parking area behind the bakery also held the dumpster and a big composter Sabrina was fanatical about. The back screen door was shut, but the storm door was open and a welcoming light and smell were coming out from it.

As well as the sound of Lady Gaga. My sister's time in Los Angeles had nearly ruined her sense of music. Luckily Lady Gaga came out with a suitable country album and "Million Reasons" was blasting from the kitchen.

I opened the screen door and poked my head inside. "Hello?" I said.

Sabrina popped up from behind one of the stainless-steel worktables. "Bea!" She actually smiled to see me and I felt myself smile back. 'What are you doing here?" she asked.

It would have been so easy to lie. I'd been lying to Sabrina my whole life. Pretending something I never really felt, just to show her I didn't feel anything. "I had a...really bad day."

She actually looked like a deer in headlights. Like she was terrified I was going to need her help. She glanced around like Ronnie might magically show up to save her from this sisterly moment.

"What are *you* doing here?" I asked, saving her. "You're usually not open at this time."

She pursed her lips and I had no idea what she was thinking. For a person I'd spent half my life with, she was a total mystery. "Garrett and I had a fight and he needs to learn a lesson about taking a girl for granted."

"Garret's taking you for granted?" Seemed impossible. Garrett was a class-act Southern boy madly in love with Sabrina.

"He's thinking about it. I can tell."

"Preemptive lesson. I like it." Her hands were coated in flour and the table in front of her had rolled-out dough cut in circles. "Well, you're busy—"

"I'm not busy," she said. "I'm working on a different kind of pie crust. I added vodka. It's supposed to make it flakier."

She pulled a bottle of vodka from the shelf under the table, and because my sister never did things in half measures it was a big bottle. Of the good stuff. And our eyes met as she held it up and slowly her eyebrow lifted.

"Want to have a drink?" she asked.

"I want to get blind drunk," I said.

My sister was beautiful. It was documented in magazines like *People* and shit. But this moment, with the flour and the bottle of vodka and the happiness she wore like sunlight dress—well, she'd never been lovelier.

The vodka still in hand she looked around. "I've got some glasses," she said. " But I don't have anything to mix it with."

"Leave it to me," I said. Because there were lemons in a basket on the corner and a seven-gazillion-pound bag of sugar on the far bench.

Within twenty minutes we were drinking Lemon Drops out of coffee mugs and eating a baked piecrust dripped in whipped cream she'd had in the walk-in cooler.

"What happened to you?" she asked, with whipped cream stuck to her upper lip. We were both a little loose.

"What do you mean?"

"The bad day. And...you've been crying."

"What? Don't be ridiculous—"

"Bea," she said. "You and Ronnie are exactly alike. Your face holds on to your tears long after you're done crying."

"That's...kind of beautiful."

"Yeah, I'm a real poet," she said with a sigh. "What happened? No, wait, let me guess. You gave all the inheritance to some asshole guy who gives good head and now you need money?"

Her eyes were bright as she sipped out of her coffee mug. And this is what we did. She took a shot and then I'd take a shot right back and then we'd be fighting. For our entire lives that's what we'd done. And I was too damn tired.

"Don't," I said. "Please."

The coffee cup paused on the way up to her mouth and she put it down again. "Bea. I'm sorry."

"I know, usually this is our thing. But I can't fucking do it tonight. Okay?"

"Of course. Yeah. I'm sorry. Tell me...what happened?"

It took two mugs full of booze and more than my half of the piecrust. But I told her. I told her about Cody. About what we did at dawn and then what we'd done in the afternoon. How I lied to him. And how I liked him.

"Wait a second...not to get caught up on the details here, but you..." She circled her hand around her crotch.

"Don't be a prude."

"In public?"

"In the extreme privacy of my side deck. And he stands behind the oak, and it's all really secretive."

Sabrina's eyes were wide open. "That's hot."

I laughed. "Yeah. It was. And now it's over and I fucked it all—"

"Hey," she said, her face real stern all of a sudden. "No. Unless you didn't tell me the whole truth, Cody fucked this up. I mean, he fucked up his share of it. Don't take it all on your shoulders."

"But Sabrina. I'm lying to him."

"Yeah. And that's bad. You should tell him the truth. Or not, whatever. But don't excuse what he did. He can't put one hand down your pants and shove you away with the other hand."

Holy shit. That's exactly what he'd done.

"That's pretty wise."

"You know," she sat up straighter on the other end of the table, "no one tells me that enough." Probably because she didn't show off her wisdom enough. She hid behind a persona she'd created. There were a lot of things she didn't show off because she thought the world would laugh at her. And I knew that because I was one of the people who'd laughed at her.

"I'm really sorry," I said. "For all those years—"

"Can we not?" she asked.

"You don't want me to apologize?"

"Sure. Yes. Of course, you were a bitch to me. But I was a bitch to you. It was mutual destruction. And I've been waiting all year for us to just...put it behind us. We're here in this town and it seems like we should be friends."

Friends. So many damn friends.

"You want to be friends. With me?"

"You're the second coolest girl in town, Bea. Of course I want to be friends."

"Then we're friends." I chinked glasses with her. "Apologies given and accepted. Moving on."

"Moving on." Her smile was not the one from the magazines. It was the one that bunched up her eyes. Made her cheeks all round and fat. It was the smile her husband got. And Ronnie. All of a sudden and out of nowhere, we just sort of snapped into place. *You're my people,* I thought. *And I'm yours.*

"So," she said and took another sip of her drink. "Do you like him?"

"Cody?"

"Is there another him?"

I shook my head, because it seemed in my life there'd never been anyone like Cody. Ever.

"Then you should try."

"He just pushed me away," I said incredulously.

"You watch. He'll apologize the first time you see him."

"I don't know—"

"Trust your wise half sister Sabrina."

"Okay, but you're going to be wrong," I said with a laugh.

"But you don't want me to be," she said. And that was the truth, as bright and real as any I'd ever known. I wanted Cody and I wanted him to apologize and I wanted us to have a chance. A real chance. Because...fuck...I had a sense we could make each other happy. All that chemistry we had, there had to be something real in there, too. Something sustaining. Because I'd never felt like this for anyone else.

"I'll tell him the truth," I said. "Tomorrow."

"Right after he apologizes."

We tapped our coffee mugs together and sipped. But Sabrina found her glass empty. "More, bartender." She held out her mug to me and I hopped off the table to go make some more simple syrup and squeeze some more lemons.

My entire soul was buoyant with possibility.

"Hey," I said, measuring sugar into a pot of water. "I have...a business proposition for you."

"I'm all ears."

That stung and I turned to give her a dirty look over my shoulder only to find that she wasn't being sarcastic. She sat there, her face all open and earnest. She was taking me seriously.

I turned back to the pot of water, blinking the burning feeling from my eyes. "You know Jack is renovating The Bar. He's expanding and fixing up the kitchen. I'm loaning him money so he can get a proper chef."

"Smart."

"Right?" I asked, over my shoulder again.

"People are smarter about food than they've ever been, even in Dusty Creek. They will pay for something delicious and they'll come back for more."

"Well, I was thinking the dessert menu could come from you. Slices of cake. Those lemon bars you do. Even something like this," I pointed at the decimated piecrust and whipped cream.

"Oh, my god, what a good idea," she said.

"You think?"

"I totally do!"

There was this balloon feeling in my chest. Like if I stood still I might float up to the ceiling. Pride. This was pride. It had been so long since I'd felt it.

"So, you're going to be part owner of The Bar?"

"No," I shook my head and twisted lemons on the juicer and then threw the wrung-out peels into her compost bin.

"What do you mean? You're giving him money to get a decent chef. You're coming up with ideas for the dessert menu and...you're giving him money."

"It's a loan. That's all. He needs money and I have it."

"Don't you care?" she asked.

"What does that mean? Of course, I care."

She shrugged like nothing was a big deal, but Sabrina had spent years in Hollywood, mastering the nuances of a shrug. "Just seems like he could use some help, too. And you could do this in your sleep."

"Are you forgetting what happened with Travis?"

"No. And before Travis took all your money you had a great idea for a bar and restaurant. I would have gone to that bar and restaurant."

"Shut up."

"I would have gone, Bea. Because it was going to be great. The Bar won't be what you were planning with Travis. But it could be its own great thing. And you could have a part of it."

I put the simple syrup in the freezer to cool it down so we weren't drinking hot martinis.

"You know it's why I opened this bakery. So I could have something of my very own. So I could show people and myself that there was more to me than being a dumb joke in a reality TV show and there was more to me than being a King."

"I want that," I said. The words with their own life. "I want to be more than the fuck-up King sister."

Sabrina shrugged. "Seems like you've got your chance."

I took the mix out of the freezer and went back to

making drinks. Eased up on the vodka because both of us had stuff to do tomorrow. "Wait a second," I said, handing her the mug. "If I'm the second coolest person in Dusty Creek, who could possibly be the first?"

"Me, dummy."

18

B EA

THE DOGS WOKE ME UP, and even though I had a little bit of a Lemon Drop hangover, I couldn't help feeling...hopeful. Really and truly hopeful. I had a plan. I had a goal.

And I was going to get Cody to see me. Really see me. I was going to apologize and he would, too, for how he'd treated me and then we'd start again. Fresh. I even planned on introducing myself to him. Shaking his hand like we'd never met.

He was going to be pissed, but he would come around.

How could he not? This thing between us was undeniable.

After the dogs peed and I poured the kibble I stood at the screen door and saw movement in the yard behind the tree. My hands went numb and I turned to get a better look.

He was there. Behind the tree. I saw his red shirt. His dark-blue jeans.

And all my hope from yesterday curled up on itself. Exhausted from the effort of trying to stay alive under all this bullshit. And growing cold from the reality that...well, he must not have cared all that much about me, after all.

We'd made no promises, but still...it hurt. This moment hurt.

I set the kibble bowls down on the floor. Thelma gave me some significant side-eye but Louise was too hungry to care. There was no way I was stepping out onto that deck. Not with him out there. I couldn't be this person to him. Not after yesterday.

I could go out there and tell him, I thought. Wipe the slate clean. But I didn't know how badly I wanted that fight right now. My jealousy of myself made my heart hurt.

Maybe we didn't have the power to make each other happy. Maybe...maybe all we could do was hurt each other.

I wore my capri yoga pants and a blue T-shirt that slipped off my shoulder and I tried really hard not to think about him. I had that meeting with Jack to talk about the loan. I'd told my sister to come in, too. Ballsy, maybe, but she'd inspired me last night.

Or maybe it had been the vodka.

Who would have thought it would be Sabrina who would inspire me to try and reach for something more? Whatever, I would take it.

And under no circumstances was I going to go outside and show Cody anything. I wasn't going to talk to him. I wasn't going...to do anything.

"Hey!" someone yelled from outside and I knew immediately who it was. "Hey!"

Pebbles hit the window of my tiny kitchen that faced out onto the backyard.

Good god, he was throwing rocks against my window, and if he did again—

He did it again and the dogs went nuts. Nails scrabbling against the hardwood floors. Louise barking up a storm. Thelma went into the kitchen and tried to get up on the counter and knocked my French press onto the floor.

"I know you're there!" he cried and more pebbles scattered against my window.

I threw open the sliding glass door and the dogs launched themselves outside, barking at Cody down in the backyard.

"Come out," he said.

What was he doing, sucking my clit one night and wanting to see some other woman's clit the next morning? And, yes, I understood I was the same person, but he didn't know that.

"Or just...let me know you're okay. It's weird, I know, but it's after seven and I worried."

And that was a fine way for this to end. I liked ending relationships with the kind of explosions that left no one alive. Much less any feelings we might still have. Yeah, this was going to be the kind of scorched-earth finale that spoke to my soul.

Because fuck him. And fuck me, too.

I stepped out onto my porch and there he was, back in his usual spot on the other side of that fucking tree. Maybe this was actually all the tree's fault. Giving us just what we needed to act like fools.

"You're okay," he said.

I held out my arms as if to say—take a look.

"This is our last morning," he said, and I felt all my

anger dissipate and I wanted to clutch it back so I wouldn't do what I already knew I was going to do. His voice was dark and hard, and I told myself it was because he was sad about this being the end. That he was all cut up about it.

And maybe a little cut up about what he'd done to his friend yesterday. But I stopped that thought as soon as I had it. I didn't need to tell myself lies.

"Our last chance," he said. "Goodbye. Kinda."

I didn't answer, dragging this out as long as I could until he was walking away and the smart thing to do was let him go. But I'd never been good with the smart thing to do. I took off my shirt and tossed it into the yard.

I heard him stop. Saw him stop a few feet from the tree, reach down, and pick up my sweatshirt. When he looked up, I wasn't sure of that angle so I sat way back in the chair.

"Let me see you," he said.

I let my silence be my answer.

"Your name, then."

More silence.

"I've been calling you my Morning Girl."

I said nothing.

"You know I could take three steps." He stepped forward, getting closer to the deck with every one. And I kept leaning back, making sure he couldn't see me.

"What do you want?" he asked.

Everything. I want everything.

"What do you want?' I shot back, scared of the answer.

"To see your face."

He wanted the impossible. He wanted what would ruin everything. I said nothing.

"I want to watch you. One last time."

Yeah. That's what I wanted, too. And maybe if I thought too hard about it I'd be pissed at him for wanting this so soon after he'd wanted me last night. But this felt so far out of our hands. Out of our control. This was a rock rolling downhill.

I didn't move until he stepped back to the other side of that tree. I couldn't see him at all, except for my sweatshirt thrown over his shoulder, and I liked that. Liked that a lot.

I sat down. And spread my legs out wide. And waited.

And because Cody was no dummy and it seemed like, in this, we were of the exact same mind—he caught on fast.

"Stand up," he said. "I can't...see you in the chair. Not the way I want to."

I stood, imagining what he had seen or not seen before and wondering, briefly, why this was different. He wanted more of me than he'd ever had. He was being greedy.

He'd never shown me this side of himself and I liked it. His anger and his greed.

"Take off your pants," he said, his voice stiff and hard. A little, I imagined, like his cock. I'd touched it so briefly last night. Not enough. I'd had such plans for that cock.

But I did what he asked, bending over so I could pull the black stretchy material down under my ass and off my legs. But I kept my legs closed because if he wanted anything, he was going to have to ask for it.

"You're so fucking good at this," he said. "Such a tease."

Only for you, I thought and it sent a thrill through me. This private thing I did only for him.

"Put your foot up on your chair."

Good boy, I thought, and did as he told me. The silence that followed was long. And pronounced. I started to shift my foot down from the chair.

"Don't you dare move," he said.

Oh, god, he sounded so mean. So fierce. Like he had

yesterday, pushing me up against that door. I shook a little with it all.

"Show me," he said. "Spread yourself for me."

I slipped my fingers between my lips and spread them wide until the pink skin of my labia and the hard knot of my clit were touched by the cool air. I didn't know if he could see me, it seemed totally unlikely, but it hardly mattered.

"You like it when you squeeze your clit. When you do that to yourself, you skin goes pink and all the muscles in your stomach clench. Do that. Squeeze your clit between your fingers. Just the way you like it."

Oh, he was a noticing kind of man. And I dearly appreciated that about him. Right now, perhaps more than ever. I did what he said, because he was right and I did like it and I gasped loud enough that he could hear it.

"Tease yourself with your fingers. You like that too. Just the tip of your finger inside your body and then pull it out, slower and deeper each time."

And so, I did it, slow and deep and everything just the way I liked it.

"Tell me your name."

I stopped and closed my legs and even that pressure lit me up.

"Yeah," he said, all dark and grim. "That's what I thought. Are you wet?" he asked, and I nodded.

"Tell me," he said.

"Yes. I'm wet."

"You have a birth mark," he said, and I stopped. I actually stopped breathing. I dropped my leg so he couldn't see it. The little brownish-red spot right there on the inside of my thigh. You had to be really up close and personal to see it and I wondered if he'd seen it last night. Or before.

"I noticed it before," he said. "I don't know why I said anything."

Because, I feared, he was starting to put two and two together. Because I'd slipped maybe one too many times. If he wanted to see what was right in front of his face, it was undoubtedly there. But he was blinded by his own stuff. And it was shitty of me to judge him because I'd been blinded by my own stuff, too. It was how this started.

"I want you to come," he said. "I want to hear it and see it, and if I was a different kind of guy you wouldn't be able to stop me from coming up there to taste it."

He'd liked going down on me. The head that man gave was dedicated and next-level.

I slipped my fingers back between my legs. I was slick and hot and perfect. I moaned so he knew how much I liked what he was saying.

"You would taste so sweet. So sweet and I would lick you and suck you until it hurt, just a little. Because you like it hard." Again, somehow proving how well he knew me from twenty feet away. "You like it to hurt just a little. And I can make you hurt just right, baby."

I cried out, a low pained sound, because he was pulling me apart with his words. With all of it.

No more. "I can't take it." I didn't mean to say that, but words like the sweat and the come just poured out of me.

"You can."

"Cody," I cried. And then I exploded. Shaking and sobbing. I jerked my hands away from myself because it was all too fucking much, and when I stopped heaving in breaths, I noticed that, in the back, it was silent.

I could see him there, but he didn't say anything. And he didn't have his cock out. What...happened?

"How do you know my name?"

Did I say his name? I must have said his name. Fuck.
What would it matter if he found out? Now on the other
side of this anger, on the other side of pretending once again
that we were just this and not an entirely other thing as well.
I knew in my gut he'd be so upset. He'd feel betrayed.

He'd...hate me.

"Jack," I said.

"How long have you known my name?" he asked.

"Not long," I lied.

I hummed in my throat and pulled up my pants, the air
suddenly cool with all this emotional nudity. I was a mess.
In my head. Between my legs. I needed a shower and a firm
talking-to from my sister. God, where was Ronnie when I
needed her?

"Hey." His voice sounded different, closer and when I
looked down at the yard, he wasn't in his spot. "I'm here."

I followed the sound of his voice and he was right there.
Practically right beneath me. The angles were different and
his eyes were looking right into my eyes.

It was shocking seeing him like that. So close. No tree
hiding us. I jumped, like he'd startled me. Like I had a
chance of hiding from him again. But it was over. All over.

No. Oh, God. No.

19

"**B**ea." That was all he said. My name. Like a curse.

"I can...I can explain. Come up and we can talk—"

"I don't want to talk."

"Cody!"

"Was it fun?" he asked. "This fucking game of yours? Did you have a good time?"

"It wasn't like that. I swear."

He just shook his head at me and then walked away, out of sight. Under my porch toward his truck and out of my life for—I was sure—forever.

I raced through my apartment, grabbing a shirt as I went, and hurtled down my steps, catching him at the street near his truck.

"Let me explain," I said. His eyes raked over me and I felt naked in my clothes. I felt bruised. I had never been scared of him, not once.

But now I was.

"Were you ever going to tell me?" he asked. "Just now...I gave you, like, ten chances to come clean."

"I know. I meant to tell you. I wanted to tell you."

"Did you tell Jack not to tell me who you were?"

I nodded.

"Before or after you knew who I was?"

"After. But I was going to tell you."

"All that matters is you didn't, Bea. Why?"

"Because it was the only way I could be with you."

He shook his head and looked away like he couldn't stand the sight of me.

"You know what I did last night?" he asked, and I shook my head, my tongue too swollen to use. "Counted up all the times you lied to me. To my face. I couldn't even count the times you could have told me the truth but decided not to."

"Cody—" I reached for him and he shrugged me off.

"I thought we were friends," he spat.

I jerked back. "Which girl were you friends with? The woman you kicked out of your house yesterday? Or the woman you like to watch come every morning, but went out of your way to not see her face?"

"Don't make this about me," he said.

"It's all about you. It's all about trying to figure out how I could be close to you. Because you put so much shit in my way. What was yesterday, Cody? What the fuck happened at your house?"

He yanked open the door to his truck and I jumped in front of it.

"I liked you. And I lied so I could be in your life. Because I thought we had something special—"

"And if it was some other guy out there that first morning, watching you bend over on that deck, would you think he was special?"

I gasped. He looked away, his jaw tight.

"I don't deserve that," I said. I pressed my hand to my

stomach because it hurt so much. I felt like I was going to vomit.

"Yeah," he said. "You do." He put his hands on my shoulders and carefully pushed me aside. And my skin soaked up even that contact like a sponge. "It feels like you pulled part of my life out from under me. Like I don't know what the fuck is going on. I sure as hell don't know who you are."

He walked around me, but I grabbed his arm and held on when he tried to shake me loose. "What I felt for you was real. And what you felt for me was real, too."

He looked at me like I was dirt. Pure filth. "Nah," he said. "I think we scratched an itch. Go find some other fool to play your games with."

He left and I staggered forward, like I'd had my legs kicked out from under me. He drove away, leaving me in the dust. I made my way upstairs on legs that barely worked and once inside my apartment I fell down on my knees.

Distressed by my distress, the dogs came over to lick my tears, of which there was an endless supply.

I DON'T KNOW what time it was when my phone rang. I'd moved from my floor to my bed and the dogs were providing as much care as they could.

"Hello," I said into the phone.

"Hey." It was Jack. "You coming? We're supposed to be meeting."

"What time is it?" I asked.

"Well, you're a half hour late for our meeting and it's almost time for your shift to start."

"Jack," I sighed.

"Are you sick? You okay?"

No. No. My heart is broken. My pride is ravaged. I'm a fucking disaster.

I felt the swell of my excuses rise up in my chest. The old litany of shit I could say.

I should quit. Right now. Save myself that hassle of doing it later.

Save Jack the pain of trusting me and then having me fail him. It would be so easy to make up excuses for how I never really liked that place anyway. And those plans I'd been making for the expansion and the future, I never really wanted those plans.

I started to do what I always did—fail everyone.

Fail myself.

"I'm coming." I sat up in bed, startling the dogs.

"You sure, because if you're sick—"

"I'm not. I just...give me twenty minutes."

Twenty minutes to get my shit together.

Thirty minutes later I was downstairs for my meeting with Jack. I wore a pair of dress pants with heels and a button-up shirt that was a little too tight. I looked like a bank teller in a porno. It was kind of a costume and I needed it to keep my shit together.

It gave my fake-it-until-you-make-it desperation something to cling to.

"Bea," Jack said, "Are you okay? Because, no offense, you look...not well."

"You say that to all the girls?" Lame, so lame, but I was barely keeping it together.

"Hey," Jack said, scanning up and down. He put his fingers through his belt loops and gave me a cheesy grin. Playing along like he knew that's what I needed him to do. "You want me to make a deposit."

"For your information, I was going for banker-in-a-porno as my look."

"Well, mission accomplished," he said. "Though—"

"I know. I'm not your type." I tilted my head and looked at him closely. "What's your look?" He was wearing a button-down shirt. And a pair of dark jeans. His beard was even trimmed. I leaned over and sniffed him. He smelled like expensive beard oil.

"Nervous investee," he said.

"You don't need to be nervous," I said. "I'm a sure thing."

"Don't..." He shook his head. "Don't make jokes that sell yourself short. If you do this for me, you're changing my life. You're changing the fucking town. If you can't take yourself seriously, at least take that seriously."

"Right," I said, sobered by his words. Sometimes I just had to be shown the way out of my own way. Usually that was what Ronnie did for me, constantly pushing me out of my ruts. And I'd come this far without her. I could do the rest. "Of course."

"I have, like, a proposal thing I found online," he said and handed me two pieces of paper stapled together. "It's got what I plan to do with the place. What I'd use your money for and some information on what the bar was pulling in per month."

"Holy shit! That much?"

"I know. But I'm the only bar in town with chairs. Imagine if The Bar was actually nice."

"We're gonna make a killing."

"Here," he said and pointed at another section of his proposal. "This is how I'll repay you. Interest, etc. and here," his hand slid down the form to the very bottom, "is what we agreed on. Price-wise."

"This is all awesome. Really, Jack. So awesome. I'll run out to the bank today and get you a suitcase of cash."

"A check will do."

"Nah. I'm gonna get you a burlap bag with a big money sign on it."

"Is this the kind of humor I can look forward to for the entire project?"

"Yep." I put the paper down on the bar. "But I had another idea—"

Of course, at that moment my sister walked in looking like a million dollars in a yellow dress and pretty red flats. Her hair was up high in a bouncy ponytail. She had that natural makeup look down cold. And she made my banker porno look seem even worse.

"Hey," she said. "Bad time?"

"Perfect time."

"What's going on?" Jack asked.

"My sister is part of my idea," I said. "Have a seat. Let's talk."

CODY

I HAD to do therapy after the accident. Not just the physical stuff, but mental. A shrink came into my hospital room and just "wanted to talk." She asked bullshit questions about how I felt not being in the rodeo anymore.

I'd been through a lot of this before, so I knew there were three kinds of answers. The honest kind that would lead to more bullshit talking. The lying kind, which would lead to more bullshit talking. And the answers that lay somewhere in the middle. The answers that managed to let in all the ghosts I didn't like thinking about, but ultimately made the shrink put a signature on the form and leave me the fuck alone.

With the ghosts I didn't want let out.

But the shrink was pretty smart. And she'd caught on to what I was doing and told me that I should pay attention to when I was being defensive, because it usually meant that deep down I was scared.

"You've seen my record," I'd said, looking down at her lap. "I'm not scared of shit."

"Oh, Cody," she said. "You're scared of everything."

Well, that made me super defensive. And as I drove up to the ranch where Bonnie was being kept I was raging with defensiveness. I was purely pissed off.

Fucking Charlie.

Fucking Bea.

Jesus Christ, I hadn't even recognized myself this morning with her. I'd never spoken to a woman like that. Of course, I'd never been hurt by a woman like that.

Not since my mother, which told me plenty about how I'd let it go too far with Bea.

Way too fucking far.

When I'd realized who she was last night, sitting in the dark drinking that beer she'd left behind, I wondered if I'd somehow known that they were the same person. Some place deep in my snake brain I must have known, because I couldn't explain how I'd let my guard down so completely with two different women. How open I'd made myself in totally different ways. And how I couldn't even show one person that much of myself.

Unless she'd somehow tricked me.

And then I just got mad. And stayed mad.

When I saw her again, well, I needed to apologize, and

then I'd stay as clear of her as I could in this town. Which wouldn't be easy, but I'd done plenty of hard things before.

I parked at the far edge of the lot that was full of fancy cars and trucks. I recognized Charlie's old Denali and felt like I was going to have an aneurysm. I had to calm down before I went in there. Before I saw Bonnie and the old man.

Or I'd stroke out in the barn.

Outside the truck the day was hot and getting hotter but there were big poplars in between all the buildings casting a nice shade. The corrals were full of horses being worked out, nice and slow. There was a pretty black mare limping around the circle and I had to look away.

The blast of the air conditioning inside the reception area turned all the sweat on my lower back into icicles.

"Can I help you?" the receptionist asked, and the instinct to run was nearly out of my control.

"Yeah. I'm Cody McBride. I'm here for—"

"Bonnie!" She said, smiling wide like I was family just arrived for Christmas dinner. "Of course. What a sweetheart she is. And a fighter, my goodness!"

"Yeah," I said through a lump in my throat. "That would be her."

"The doctor and Charlie Hoynes are already out at the barn. You can join them through there." She pointed to a glass side door and I quickly made my escape out into the sticky Texas heat. Sweat gathered in my hairline and ran down my spine. There was nothing really to be prepared for. I'd last seen Charlie in the hospital and that was just a few months ago. It was only Charlie, after all, but when I stepped into the wide-open door of that stable and my eyes adjusted to the murk, it felt like I'd been pulled from that horse all over again.

Charlie. Jesus Christ. In that old brown suit and that

beat-up hat. He was six foot and three hundred pounds of pure old-school Texas.

He was the closest thing I have ever had to a father. By a mile.

My vision swam and that aneurysm felt imminent.

"Mr. McBride," the other man said. The doctor or whatever. "Glad you could make it."

I shook his hand and didn't give Charlie a glance, but could feel his attention. And his disapproval.

Leave it, Charlie, I thought. *I'm just trying to survive this shit.*

"I was telling Mr. Hoynes that Bonnie's recovery has been miraculous, really. We weren't sure for the first month if she'd survive the injury. We managed to treat her physically but she remained in a withdrawn state. Horses are herd animals and being solitary can often lead to depression, so we made sure Bonnie was surrounded by other horses. We even put one of the barn cats in her stall. But nothing seemed to pull her out of that withdrawn state."

"Yeah," Charlie muttered. "I wonder what she was missing."

I didn't look at him, and the guilt I was trying not to feel was crushing me. I could barely breathe. "But she's all right now?"

"She is. We put her in a stall next to another rodeo horse. An older stallion who'd gone blind in one eye, and I don't know..." The doctor smiled. "Maybe they told old war stories at night, but the stallion pulled her out of it."

"That's good. That's...real good." I managed to say. Bonnie got better because she was competitive and if that old blind warhorse was on its feet—goddammit, she would be, too.

"Would you like to go see her?" the doctor aske-, all

bright eyed and happy at the idea of reuniting me with my old horse. It was a YouTube video dream come true. He could Instagram it and make it a Facebook story or some shit—get a million clicks of my horse and I seeing each other for the first time since the accident.

"No," I said. "That's all right."

The doctor looked confused and I didn't have the will to explain all the reasons why I couldn't look into Bonnie's eyes. And there was some kind of chance she wouldn't be happy to see me.

"Hey, doc," Charlie said. "Give us a minute, would you?"

"Of course. I'll be in Bonnie's stall, just around the corner," he said and walked away into the labyrinth that was this giant stable.

"Charlie," I said, trying to cut him off before he could start. "Don't—"

But he surprised me by shoving me with his considerable strength. I stumbled back. My shoulders hit the wall behind me and tackle fell off a hook by my head.

"Charlie, what the hell?"

"I may be thirty years older than you, punk, but I can still knock you down a peg." He pushed that old hat up on his wide forehead and got right up in my face. I looked away but he wouldn't let me. "I've let you wallow in this shit enough, boy."

Oh, god. We were going with *boy* again.

"It's time you dragged yourself up out of this withdrawn state—"

"Will you stop?"

"No."

"I have a job, Charlie. A good one that could grow into something big. And you know what? I like it. I'm okay. I have friends, too. Real ones." Well, I might be down a friend after the other day. Bea would have every right never to speak to me again. "I know you want me to be destroyed because I can't rodeo anymore, but guess what? I've moved on."

"That's why you aren't returning my calls?"

"What do we have left to say, Charlie? I told you I'd pay you back—"

"I don't want your fucking money."

"Then why do you keep fucking calling?" I shoved him back, stepping away from the wall where he had me pinned with his bulk. It wasn't smart, going after Charlie, he was a dirty-fighting son of a bitch. But I wasn't going to be backed into a corner.

"I'm calling about you. About how you're doing. About how your life is going."

"Just great." I didn't mean to sound sarcastic but it was how it came out.

He sighed and glanced away, his hands on his hips. "I just want to help."

A cold chill ran down my back and I realized what was happening. Why Charlie kept coming back. It was because I was giving him a fight. I needed to answer him like I answered that shrink. Just enough honesty to get him to leave me the fuck alone.

"You did help," I said. "You believed in me when no one else did and Charlie, we had some good times. Some...really good times. And I was happy to wear your sponsorship. I was proud of it." Fuck. My voice was getting thick. This was too much honesty. "But rodeo is behind me."

"You saying after all those years together, all those miles, we were nothing but rodeo? It was me with the money and you in the ring, and that's it? That's all? Because son—"

"Yep," I said, fast and hard. Because that *son* always fucking broke me. "That's all."

"So, you're putting me and Bonnie out to pasture. Goodbye and good riddance?"

"What else is there to do?"

Charlie looked at me a long time and I forced myself to look right back. "I keep forgetting how feral you were when I found you."

"Shut up, Charlie."

"How you didn't know how to disagree with someone without putting a fist in their face. And you didn't know how to be a friend with someone—"

"I have friends."

"No, you don't," he said in that emphatic way that said he knew better. "You have girls you fuck until they break their heart over you, and you had your gran, that kid Jack, and you had me. You telling me that's all changed?"

Did Bea break her heart over me? Or did I break mine over her? Either way, neither of us walked away from what happened between us intact.

"I call you because I care, Cody. I know you don't like it when I call you son."

"I'm not your goddamned son."

"But you are," he whispered. "To me you are. And you're breaking my heart leaving me in the cold like this."

It was like someone was squeezing my chest in a fist. Things were breaking up and crumbling. It felt like I was honestly going to die.

"You never have to pay me back, son. You just have to let me in."

"Where?" I whispered. "To what? I'm living in my Gran's house. Working construction and killing myself trying to get a forty-five percent bend back in my knee. What part of that do you want?"

"All of it."

"Charlie." I laughed. "You've got a gazillion-dollar oil company to run."

"It runs itself. I'm sorry your momma taught you that you weren't interesting unless you were in the spotlight."

"Don't," I whispered because I couldn't take it anymore. I really couldn't.

"But me and Bonnie deserve better than what you've given us. And you know it. Because me and that horse gave you everything we had."

Oh, God, it was so fucking true. I turned away because my face was hot and my chest was so tight I couldn't take a full breath without it shaking my whole body. "I feel like I failed you," I finally said. "And I know I failed Bonnie. She did everything I asked of her and she nearly died, and I don't know how to make that better."

"First thing you do is go walk into that stall. Let her get a good nose full of you. You'll see she carries no grudges. And neither do I, son."

Charlie half-led, half-pushed me around the corner to the stall. I kept my eyes on my boots because I was putting off looking at her for as long as I could. There was a rhythmic pounding up ahead. The sound of a horse beating its chest against a stable door. A couple of the hands came trotting past me towards the horse in distress. I heard her, that deep whinny, and out of instinct I looked up to see it was her pounding herself against that stall.

And those big brown eyes looked right at me. I stopped, the two of us staring at each other, and then she was tossing that head and lifting her front legs, beating at the at door like she was going to knock it down. Her whinny got higher and more distressed and I couldn't stand it.

I ran the last few feet and got my hands on her neck and

she put her nose right in my chest, breathing me in with big pulls of her magnificent lungs.

"Hey there," I whispered and her ears flicked. "Hey, sweetheart." I kept talking nonsense to her, telling her how amazing she was. How strong. How brave.

She put her nose against my chest and then my face, her lips nuzzling the collar of my shirt, and I stroked the soft white-and-brown-spotted neck and I didn't realize I was crying until I tasted the salt of my tears on my lips.

And all that praise I whispered to her turned into, "I'm sorry. I'm so sorry," in her ear on steady repeat. I was vaguely aware of Charlie talking to the doctor, signing some paperwork, and I was happy to let him handle it because Bonnie needed to be told she was such a good horse, such a good girl, and that I wouldn't leave her alone like that again. Ever again.

I ran my hands over her sides, happy to see that if she'd lost weight after the accident she'd gained it back. She looked healthy and felt strong.

My horse. My beautiful horse.

"She's a wonderful animal," the doctor finally said, interrupting our reunion.

"Yes, she is," I said.

"And Oscar out at The King's Land will take great care of her."

Oh. Right. Shit. Another situation I needed to make right.

The doctor left and it was just me, Charlie, and Bonnie, and a tabby cat in the corner watching us through half-closed eyes.

"Thank you, Charlie," I said, because it was the only thing to say.

Charlie nodded and I saw his own eyes were damp. And

man, I didn't know a lot about friendship. About what happened when one person was in pain and the other one just had to stand there and watch it all go down. But it couldn't be easy. "I'm sorry I put you through all this."

He took a deep breath, the pearl snaps of the shirt beneath that sport coat of his earning their money trying to keep his chest inside the fabric. "Buy me a beer and we'll call it even."

"Sure thing," I said with a laugh. "But I gotta get Bonnie out to The King's Land."

"I brought my trailer. We can hook it up to your truck."

"Like the old days," I said. Remembering when he first sponsored me in the shit circuit in Oklahoma. I was sleeping in my truck, borrowing money from Gran to pay my entrance fees. He came up to me after a big all-around win and told me he couldn't stand to see a man live like this. Sponsored me for five thousand dollars.

It was more money than I'd ever had in my life.

And for the cost of five grand some days he'd ride with me in my truck, from arena to arena across the Panhandle. The two of us decimating a bag of sunflower seeds and talking shit.

How could I have forgotten those days? How could I have treated this man so poorly?

"Charlie," I whispered and shook my head, the words to big to make their way out of my chest.

"It's all right, son. Let's take care of Bonnie and you can get me that beer," Charlie said, clapping me on the back.

This time the *son* felt good.

It felt right.

20

B EA

THE DOGS and I were driving out to The King's Land.

It was part of an elaborate plan to make sure I didn't think about Cody. So far, in order to not think of Cody, I'd cleaned my house. Painted my toes. Made some calls to Austin and Houston about poaching some kitchen staff, got a bead on a young man I liked to be our chef.

And I came to grips with the fact that I needed to move. For real. It was criminal keeping those dogs in a one-room apartment. We needed a yard. Fenced in with a tree for shade. And I didn't care what came with it. A house. Apartment. I'd take a camper if I had to. But these poor dogs needed a place to roam. A tree to lie under.

"I'm sorry guys," I yelled over the radio and they both jumped up to lick my face. Absolving me because that was what pets did. Bonnie, for all Cody's imagined crimes, probably did the horse equivalent of this. Lapped at his shirt, butted her head into his chest. Searched for contact. Offered up the same.

I sighed, feeling grief in my belly for a man I didn't want to feel a damn thing for.

I grabbed my phone and had my thumb over Ronnie's number to see if she knew any real estate agents or, really, to see if she had any ideas where I should live and I stopped. Because that instinct was another thing that had to end. She couldn't solve my problems for me.

I wasn't going to call Sabrina, either.

Instead I pulled over on Old Flagg Road and searched local real estate agents, found a woman whose face I liked and who had pretty good Google reviews, and I called her and made an appointment with her for Monday.

Because I was an adult goddammit.

And it was time for me to act like one.

I PULLED in under the gates at The King's Land only to find the parking area fuller than usual. Some giant Denali and a horse trailer. The bottom of my stomach got cold with a sense of foreboding. Shit.

Shit. Shit. Shit.

Cody was here. He was dropping off Bonnie. I could feel it across my skin and the pit of my belly. For a moment I considered turning around and heading back into town. But I wasn't going to have Cody push me away from my own damn house.

I stopped on the far side of the parking area and Thelma jumped and Louise whined until I got her down.

Something smelled good from inside the house so the dogs took off that way.

I walked inside the house I hated without really looking around. But it was hard not to notice what was being done. Maria was boxing shit up. It was, in fact...almost all gone. My step-mother's modern glass collection that looked like a thousand variations of a dick, my father's old trophy heads and dusty old furs were off the walls and shelves. She was painting all the walls a bright, clean white.

Without all that crap, the living room—with a wall full of windows—was actually really pretty. It kind of glowed. In the kitchen, Maria was trimming fat from a pork roast and feeding it to the dogs.

The kitchen always looked good. It was all brick and copper pots and a big gas stove where Maria worked her magic.

"You'll spoil them," I said and walked over to kiss her.

"Right. Because you're so strict." She leaned her cheek into my kiss. She smelled like cumin and roses. "Why are you here?"

"Giving them a chance to run. What's going on outside?" I asked. The window over the breakfast table looked out at the barn. There was a pretty strawberry roan out there, trotting around one of the corrals, shaking her mane like she was putting on a show for the cowboys standing around the fence line.

Cody was there. His sweat-stained hat pushed back on his blond head.

It was ridiculous to think I could have loved him. Even while I was lying to him. Tricking him. But the thought was there, as hard and real as truth.

I could have loved him. And maybe it was delusional, but I think he could have loved me, too.

"That new horse is moving in. Oscar and I are leaving

tonight," Maria said. "Dwayne and the boys will see her settled."

"Headed to Galveston?" I asked.

"Yep. Leaving at five. Shoo, pups, I got nothing else for you," she said and then came to look out the window with me. "Pretty horse."

"Hmmm."

"Pretty cowboy." Maria caught my eye and wiggled her eyebrows.

"Dirty bird," I said and bumped her hip with mine. "Hey," I said. "I like what you're doing with the place."

"Those old things should have been gotten rid of years ago," Maria said. "And it will be easier to sell the place with all that clutter gone."

"When is it going on the market?"

"No idea. Ronnie just asked me to clear out the junk."

"Have you done the upstairs?" I asked.

"No," she grinned at me. "I was waiting for you girls to come home and clear out your own rooms. You could do that right now."

"Maria," I sighed, but she was jostling me around the shoulders. It was nice. Like something Ronnie would do.

"No, you girls have been putting it off all year. Go clean out your stuff. Throw it all away. Keep it. Whatever you want, just...go look. Nothing is as bad as you think it is."

Oh, God, wasn't that a lie. Particularly here. Everything on The King's Land was just as bad as I thought it was.

Even that cowboy out there.

Especially him.

"Okay," I agreed. Because I imagined there wouldn't be anything I wanted to keep. No mementos from my rather tumultuous childhood. Binky, my stuffed elephant, already sat on my bedside table. And I had my sisters. The rest was just...junk.

"We have to go," Maria said, looking at her watch. "I'm gonna have to drag that man away from the corral. If you want to spend the night," she said. "There are clean sheets in the master."

"Sleep in my dad's old bed?" I asked.

"Hardly looks like what it used to," Maria said. "We got rid of all that old furniture—you won't even recognize it." She kissed me on one cheek and patted me on the other and then was gone. Taking the roast wrapped up in the tinfoil with her. The dogs whined at the door she went out of.

I propped open the back door, which opened up onto the screened-in porch where my mom used to spend her evenings with Ronnie and me when we were kids. Ronnie loved it out there, but it made me uncomfortable in the way the whole house did.

Like all my happy and unhappy ghosts were watching me.

Usually I raced through this room, but I didn't today. I stood still and let the ghosts rub up against me until I felt sick from it. Or maybe it was Cody's presence making me feel sick.

Hard to say.

I pushed out the screen door, onto the small stone deck, and sat down in the lawn chair, watching Maria and Oscar climb into their brand-new camper. Maria, who was driving, honked the horn as they pulled away under the gate.

The two men still down at the corral—Cody and another man—were looking at me.

And I was torn, right down the middle, between wanting him to come up here and wanting him to leave.

Come.

Leave.

Something.

But don't hurt me anymore.

And that's when I realized it was me. Me that kept putting myself in harm's way. Me that had the power to stop being hurt. Fuck this.

And fuck him.

I got up and headed back inside.

21

CODY

"SOMETHING UP THERE CAUGHT YOUR EYE?" Charlie asked when I turned to look up at that house for the hundredth time. She was a magnet in that green dress. I couldn't not look. "That is one purely pissed-off woman."

I resettled against the fence, watching Bonnie toss her mane around and show off for me.

"Fuck you, Charlie."

"What did you do to piss that woman off?"

"Bea fucking King. I should have known better." I kicked at the dirt and resettled my hat on my head. In the process I looked over my shoulder and caught her crossing her legs, the hem of that dress fluttering around her knee. "It was all just a...game to her."

"Well, her father was known for that kind of shit."

God bless Charlie. Always a sympathetic ear. I told him

the whole story. The Morning Girl and Bea and how she played me all along. Pretending to be one thing while being something else entirely.

"The fucking kick in the gut was...I liked her. I mean, really liked her," I said.

"So, that's it?"

"What do you mean?"

"You really like her and she made a mistake and so...that's it?"

"What am I supposed to do?" I asked. I'd already decided I needed to apologize for that shit I said to her, but past that, what future did Bea King and I have?

"You can take her in," Charlie said to the hand who was walking Bonnie, and she trotted over to us as if to say goodnight. I stroked my hands over her neck, felt the familiar warmth of her twitching skin.

And then she was gone.

"I better go make sure they're not giving Bonnie—"

"You stay right there, boy," Charlie said, and his tone made me stand up straight. We faced each other next to the fence, the wind whistling through the stable doors. "A woman doesn't go to all that trouble for a trick. You're not that much of a prize, my friend."

"What the hell?"

"It's obvious you cared for her. And it's real obvious she cared for you, too, and you're not an easy man to care for," he said.

I opened my mouth to call bullshit, but I knew it was true. I'd made it impossible for her to be my friend.

"You've tried to buck me off so many times I've lost count, and before you get that back up, you know it's true."

I glanced up at the house and she was still there, radiating in that green. "And, yeah, she lied. A lot. But it sounds like she was just trying to hold on to you any way she could. Same as your Gran used to. Same as that friend of yours, Jack, used to. Same as me."

"You never lied to me," I said.

"Nope," he nodded. "And that's a really shitty thing to do to a person. And I wouldn't blame you if you couldn't get over that. But...sometimes the why matters more than we want it to."

I already knew why she lied. She told me. It was the only way she could keep me in her life. Because I kept pushing her away.

This time when I glanced back at the house Bea was gone. Her chair empty.

Shit.

Oh. Shit.

The panic I felt was pure adrenaline and I turned away from Charlie and all his very true words and started up the small grassy hill toward the house.

And the girl I had hurt more than I'd realized.

"Meet me at home," I yelled over my shoulder at him. "Key's under the mat."

"Bring back some beer and BBQ. Or breakfast—whenever you get home," he said and then ambled off. The neck of his jacket had a sweat ring around it.

"Don't have a heart attack in my grandma's house," I said and he flipped me the bird over his shoulder.

Once he was safely in his truck, no doubt with that AC cranked to 11, I turned back to that house. And Bea.

The patio door led into a dark screened-in porch that didn't seem to match the rest of the house. And from the porch I walked into a big kitchen. At the sound of me coming in, the two dogs I'd been seeing eating their breakfast every morning rushed out to greet me.

Close up they were even uglier. And the Chihuahua was growling at me.

"Hey," I said and held out my hand for them to sniff. "I'm a friend." The giant slobbering mastiff came over but the Chihuahua wasn't having it. She started to bark, and when I attempted to get around her she growled low in her throat.

Jesus, I thought, taken aback by the ferocity of this thing. The mastiff came over and sat on my boot and licked my palm as if to tell me, *Don't worry—she's like this with everyone.*

I got past the guard dog by finding an old rope chew toy and tossing it into the porch. I held open the door and both dogs ran past me. I locked the door behind them.

"Bea?" I called out. There was no answer but I knew she was in the house. I could smell her in the air. And her Jeep was still out front.

"Bea?" The rest of the house was huge but pretty nondescript. A big blank canvas. She wasn't in the living room or office so I headed up the big sweeping staircase to the second floor. One of the doors was open and I eased it open a little further to find Bea sitting on the carpet. Her green dress a puddle around her.

The walls were white and turquoise. The bed looked like a giant flower. There were trophies on the wall. From math competitions.

"Is this...your room?"

It didn't feel like her room.

"My sister's. What are you doing here?" she asked, pulling things out of a dresser and throwing them into a garbage bag. Her fury put me off my stride.

"We're moving Bonnie in."

"She settled?"

"Yeah...it's great. She's real happy."

"Your horse is happy."

"Yeah."

"Wonderful." Her sarcasm was so thick I could taste it. "You can leave."

"I want to talk."

"I don't really care what you want." She stood up and the skin of her chest was red and splotchy. She was furious, sending out sparks, and the air suddenly seemed really dry. Dangerously combustible.

"What I said the other day about you...bending over for other men—"

She looked away, her lips tight. "Fuck you for that."

"I've never talked to a woman like that in my life."

"Yeah, well, I lied to you. So...are we even?"

I didn't say anything. What would "even" look like between us? Like what we had a few days ago? Surely there was more we could have. More we could get.

"You were right," she said, running her hands along the bag she was holding. "We should have just stayed friends. Benefits always screws things up."

"Benefits didn't screw us up. I did. With my shit. And you did. With the lie."

She went completely still. Her lips parted on her breath.

Once, when I was in Oklahoma, there was this pond that froze over and Charlie dared me to go walk across it. I did, and about halfway I could hear the ice breaking beneath me. It didn't sound the way I thought it would. It sounded like a monster groaning under my feet.

This moment felt the same way.

Like a monster was about to get us.

"Then what do you want, Cody?" she asked carefully, like she was scared. Like she was on the ice with me, too.

22

"I want to kiss you," I told her.

"Sex?"

"Yes. And don't pretend you don't want that, too. No more lying."

"Fine. No lying. And then what?"

"I want to be inside you when you come."

She lifted a finger to wipe away the tear stuck to her eyelashes and then she sat there for a second, in her sister's bedroom because I knew she couldn't bear to go into her own room. In this house where she'd never been happy. I knew all of that about her. I knew so much. The lie aside, we'd been so honest with each other.

She had every right to turn me down. In fact, it would be smart for her to do it. For both of us.

But I wanted her yes. I wanted it so bad I could taste it. Taste her—salty and sweet in the back of my throat.

"And then what?" she asked.

"What do you mean?"

"We do that. I come with you inside me. And you let me touch you the way you never have. We fuck and then...do we draw straws to see who hurts the other one? Do we just take turns? You went last, so it's my turn. As long as one of us pushes the other one away so we don't have to deal with what we've done?"

"No. We don't do that."

She laughed, but it was bitter. "You sure? Because it kind of seems like our thing, Cody."

I sat down beside her, my feet stretched out until her dress touched my leg and I liked that. It might be all I ever get from her again.

"Charlie...the guy you talked to about Bonnie. He was..." I exhaled. What was the best way to describe that stubborn force of nature? "He was the closest thing I had to a dad for a long time." Dad. Yeah. That worked. That was the right word. "And after the accident I pushed him away, because I didn't know what to do with myself and all my fucked-up feelings. Because he seemed to want me to feel them all the time and I wanted to feel nothing. And he... well, he just said that you wanted to love me but I make it hard."

She flinched, went back to putting things in bags until I reached forward and forced her to stop. Actually put my hands over hers. I could feel her shaking.

"He said you were broken," she said to me. "Someone broke you and you never got fixed right."

My skin crawled all along my back and it was hard to stay still. To be in this room. But this was the price of having her. And I wanted her.

"Sounds like something Charlie would say," I finally managed to get out.

"Who broke you?"

"Well," I laughed, because my entire body was running hot and cold. "That's kind of a toss-up. "

She got to her feet and turned as if that was it. As if I'd blown it.

"Hey." It took me a second to get to my feet with my knee, but I managed to snag her arm, touching the inside of her elbow where the skin was so pink and soft. "I'm sorry. Jokes are kind of...well, it's how I cope."

"Yeah and how is that working out for you?"

"It's not. But you know that, don't you? You do the same thing."

We were a lot alike, this beautiful girl and me. I saw it more and more. And this risk I was feeling while I looked at her, standing so close. She was feeling it, too. I could see it in her eyes. The set of her shoulders. The goose bumps across her skin.

"My mom," I said, clumsy and blunt. "She...I mean, that's what the shrinks all told me, that she was the one who broke me. I got arrested when I was a kid, sent to this camp —that's where I met Jack."

"He told me."

I nodded because I figured. Jack wasn't embarrassed about his past like I was. "We had to do all this talking, you know? To get to go home. And there was all this shit I forgot about my mom when I was little."

"Like what?"

"She'd leave me alone, for days. She'd pick me up in the middle of the night and take me out to some party so I could drive her home. There was always some man she was trying to make love us and when they left it was somehow my fault. She'd show up drunk at my school, scream at me in front of my friends. And then the next day she'd do her hair and her makeup and she kiss me, and she'd be so beautiful, pretending like nothing ever happened. She'd send me to Gran's and leave me there for...weeks." I shook my head, the memories had an old brutality. They didn't hurt like they used to but they weren't exactly painless, either.

"I'm really sorry," she said.

"Yeah. But I had Gran. And Jack. And Charlie, too. She came sniffing around once I started making money and I..." God, this was hard. Way harder even than I'd thought. I looked at the old dressing table in the corner. The mirror was covered with old stickers. Stars and hearts and unicorns with silver tails.

She touched my chin, refocusing me. "What happened with your mom when you started making money?"

"She came around again. Started showing up. About a year ago, when I was making real money. Acting...like a mom. And Charlie warned me, he totally warned me, but I ignored him. Because she was my mom and she was loving on me. And I...ate it up with a spoon. I forgot every time she hurt me and every time she disappointed me. And then I got hurt and she...vanished again."

"Wait. Your mom is still alive?"

"Yeah."

"Where?"

I smiled at her fierceness, wondering where she'd been in those years. I could have used her kind of friendship. "You gonna track her down? Make her give a shit after all these years?"

"I'm not kidding," she said, all spitfire and sparks.

Her anger felt good. Like an icepack on an old injury. "Hey," I said and touched her cheek. "It's all over. I mean, as *all over* as things can get between a mother and a son. I still wade through the shit she left behind. But it's not day-to-day anymore."

"You lost everything with that accident," she whispered.

"Nope. Not even close."

Her eyebrows lifted like she didn't believe me.

"I thought that was true," I said. "And then one morning this woman stepped out on a balcony and rocked my fucking world."

"Don't—" She tried to pull away, but I wouldn't let her.

"And then the next day another woman started handing me parts of myself again, like it was shit she just found lying around. My pride and my sense of humor. My compassion. My friendship. You reminded me that I didn't lose everything. And I'll introduce you to Charlie and to Bonnie because I still have them, but only because of you, Bea. Who knows how long I would have pushed them away if it weren't for you?"

She kissed me. Up on tiptoes she grabbed hold of my shirt and kissed me. Dry. Hard. Close-mouthed. Nothing sexy about it, but all the blood in my body made a galloping run for my dick.

I wrapped my arms around her back and she went soft against me, like she was made to melt against my body. I lifted her and she opened her mouth. Spread her legs and wrapped them around my waist. She hung on me like a vine and I got as inside her as I could in that moment.

She tasted like something new in my life. Like something I wanted. Needed. And I could not, for the life of me, get enough. Bea was making an addict out of me.

I stepped toward the bed and she jerked back. "Your knee," she breathed through swollen lips. Fuck, what I was going to do with that mouth. It made me blush. It made me rock hard against the sweet, hot center of her body, and when I walked toward the bed, I rubbed her just right.

"No."

That made me stop. That made me run ice cold. I let her down my body and stepped back. Unable to look at her.

"I'm sorry," I said. "I just keep getting it wrong with you. You want to talk some more. I can keep apologizing—"

"I don't want to do it in here," she said. "This is a sad fucking room. I don't want to fuck you in a sad fucking room."

"Well, quick, find a happy one," I said.

"It's hard in this house."

"I can fuck you in every room until we make them happy."

Her face was still for a second and then she burst into laughter. "I know just where to start."

She led me down the hallway across pale carpet that felt too clean beneath my boots. I started to worry that I might mess something up. But then we were in a big open master bedroom. It smelled just a little of fresh paint and even fresher air.

Inside the door she stopped, her mouth open in wonder.

"It's totally different," she whispered. "It's...brand new."

There was a pretty four-poster bed set against a wall, covered with a bright blue duvet. She turned to look at me and then hooked a finger in the front of my jeans, tugging me behind her as she walked backward to that bed.

Everything about her, from that smile on her face to the look in her eye, told me we were about to have a real good time. And all that shit I felt, about dragging her down with me into my nonsense, it was gone. Totally gone.

"I feel happy," I said, the words and the feelings a revelation.

"Me, too," she said. But there was a lingering care, a distance I could sense in her. She wasn't ready to believe she was totally safe. She expected to be hurt after this.

I started to take off my clothes. All of them. Boots first, which took some doing. Then jeans. Shirt. Finally underwear. Until I was completely naked in front of her. My awful scars. My raging cock. Even the freckles. All there. I was skinnier than I'd ever been, but the muscle was coming back. It wasn't the body I used to have, but it was what I'd survived with.

And I would give it to her all day long.

She watched, her pale pink lips parted and wet.

"We've never been naked with each other before," I said.

She was on her feet, the dress pushed off her shoulders until she was standing in front of me with just a pair of blue cotton panties on.

And then those were gone, too.

"What's this?" I asked, touching a scar on her shoulder.

"Sabrina pushed me off a chair at dinner. I fell into the corner of the table. What's this?" she asked, running a hand along a scar on my abdomen.

"Caught the edge of a horn."

She winced.

"You're beautiful." And she was. All the pieces of her that made up the whole. That trim waist. The breasts. That look in her eye with the shrinking distance. "That was always the truth."

"You're not so bad yourself," she said with a nice little lift to her lips that made me hope we might get out of this mess yet. "You want to be inside me when I come," she said and the words made my cock jump.

"Yeah."

"Can I tell you what I want?"

Anything. Anything at all. Everything I had. Whatever she wanted.

Her hand curled around my cock and I groaned, my head falling back. The ceiling was twenty feet above me and I could have floated there when her fingers traced the flared head of my dick. The vein that ran down the top, that I'd always thought was kind of ugly, she seemed pretty interested in.

"You didn't let me touch you," she said, her voice low and husky. "And I want to touch you."

She pressed her mouth to me, breathing warm damp air across my cock. I buried my hands in her hair and pressed my legs into the insides of her thighs just so I could feel as much of her as I could.

"You gonna let me?" she asked, and I looked down only to find her watching me. Her eyes bright, her fingers toying with me. She was a vixen. A goddess.

"I'm gonna let you do whatever you want," I said.

"Yeah, you are," she sighed.

"But then..." I tightened my hands in her hair and she gasped. "It's my turn."

"What are you gonna do, cowboy?"

"Turn you inside out, baby."

She moaned low and deep in her throat and the sound was so primal, so familiar to me, I felt it in my brain. My cock jumped against her touch and she stopped teasing me. She licked me, top to bottom, sucked the tip of my cock into her mouth and I cupped her skull in my hands, the curly ends of her hair tickling my fingers and fought myself to let her do her thing.

And her thing was fucking amazing.

Her mouth was hot and wet and perfect and every time I looked down to see my cock disappearing into her face I had to work not to come. I had to force myself to keep it together. She used her hand against me, took me as deep as she could until I couldn't take anymore.

"Bea," I whispered, pushing her away.

"No," she said and cupped my ass with her hand.

"I'm gonna come."

"That's the idea." She looked up at me again, no tease, no smile. Just her swollen lips and blissed-out eyes. "Come for me."

My hands clenched around her head, dragging her back to me. Pushing myself deep into her mouth and then easing myself back, and soon she and I had a rhythm going. "Yes. God, yes, Bea. Look at you. I can't...fuck."

The orgasm rolled up my spine and exploded in my body. I jerked against her, probably pulling her hair, probably fucking her throat, and I couldn't stop myself. I emptied myself into her until I was done.

"I'm sorry," I said releasing her hair. "Did I hurt you?"

"Fuck no." She breathed and lay back against the bed. For a second all I could do was stare. As a teenager when I imagined what sex would be like, what a woman would look like—this had been it. This was the moment. She was bliss and seduction.

The most powerful thing I'd ever seen.

"What are you looking at, cowboy?" she asked, running that hand up her leg to that sweet spot between her legs.

The woman I'm falling for, I thought. *The woman I could spend my life with.*

But I didn't say any of that. She wasn't ready. We weren't ready.

So instead, I said, "You wet?" She hummed and nodded, her bottom lip between her teeth. "Show me."

She spread her legs wider and I got down on my knees in front of her and pressed my mouth right up against her. Breathing her in. Tasting her.

I licked her, sucked her until she was bowing up off the bed. Until my whole world was the scent and taste of her. I had my hand wrapped around my cock trying to keep myself from coming.

"You got condoms in this house somewhere?" I asked when I couldn't hold out any longer.

"None that are from this decade."

I pressed a kiss against her thigh, trying not to be bummed. There were a thousand things we could do.

"Hey." She lifted my chin so I was looking right into her blue, blue eyes. "I'm on the pill and I haven't had sex with anyone in a year."

"A year?"

"Travis. And I was tested after I found out he lied."

"I was tested after the accident and I sure as hell haven't been with anyone."

Her smile was slow and warm.

"I've never...been in a woman without a condom."

"Well, then this is a big day for you, isn't it?" she joked and I shook my head. Not interested in jokes. This felt big. It felt...important. She felt important.

I got to my knees on the bed, spreading her legs out wide, and when I ran my hand up to her pussy, I found her drenched.

"Jesus."

"Fuck me, Cody."

And that was it. I braced myself on my hand, notched the head of my dick to the opening of her body and slid into heaven.

"Oh, my god." She arched up into me, and when she lay back down I was deeper inside of her. She was hot, so hot. Blast furnace hot and I felt myself changed.

"Move, please." She lifted her hips again, fucking herself. Using me. And I liked that. I did. Because I liked everything this woman did. And would until the day I died. "Please, Cody."

"I like it when you beg," I whispered into her ear.

She moaned, twisting herself, lifting her leg up higher onto my back and I pushed deep inside of her. So deep her eyes popped wide and she opened her mouth to breathe like I was forcing out all the air from her lungs.

"So deep," she whispered. "You're so deep."

And I was going to get deeper. And harder. And I was going to be the last cock to feel this heat. This divine, beautiful pussy.

You're mine. Mine.

I stroked into her. Harder. Deeper.

All mine.

"Yes," she said, nodding. "Yes. Yours. I'm yours."

I'd said it out loud, revealing more than I'd intended, but the tidal wave was on us and I couldn't take it back. Wouldn't even if I could. Her chest was red above the dress and I pulled down the top until I had her breast in my hand. Her nipple in my mouth. I sucked on her and fucked her and soon we were gone. Nothing. Splintered into stardust. Together.

23

B EA

"I DON'T KNOW why you keep thinking you've hurt me," I said, trying to get up onto my elbows, but my body wasn't working. My bones and muscles and blood just needed a minute. One minute to remember what to do.

Had I ever been fucked like that? And not just the thing without the condom, though that had been hot. But that fucking intensity. Like I couldn't breathe for a few minutes there. And was still having trouble.

He'd asked me if he hurt me. And it was sweet that he cared and exciting that he didn't totally realize how into it I was. How much further we could go with this thing between us.

He was silent and when I turned his eyes were closed. He was asleep. His face was soft and relaxed. His mouth open a little. His eyelids twitching like he was having a real good dream.

I brushed the hair back from his face.

You're mine. He'd said that. Yeah, in the heat of things, but he'd said it. And I said it back and it was crazy how much I meant it. How hard I felt it in my body. Like a truth I couldn't get around.

It was scary. This feeling was like the first part of that roller coaster ride. The chug up the hill, when you were giddy with nerves, but you knew something bad was coming.

I couldn't be this happy. I couldn't actually sustain it. Something bad would happen and if it didn't—I would make it happen.

I got out of bed and cleaned myself up in the bathroom. Downstairs, I heard my phone ringing. Ronnie's ringtone. Dolly Parton's "Jolene," because sometimes if she had just the right amount to drink, she liked to sing it at the top of her lungs. I skipped my dress and instead threw on Cody's T-shirt and set a record getting down the stairs to my purse in the kitchen. I managed to get her, right before it went to voice mail.

"Ronnie!" I gasped, out of breath.

"Hey, Bea!"

"How was New York?" The dogs were whining on the porch and I opened the door, wondering how they got caught in there.

"Very good. How are you? What have you been doing the last two weeks?"

It was funny, it really was, how there was no way to answer that question. Had it really only been two weeks? How had I blown my life into so many pieces in so short a time? That had to be a new record.

"Bea?" she asked, with that tone I knew so well. She was trying not to imagine the worst while at the same time bracing herself for it. "Are you okay?"

So, of course, I did what any fuck-up little sister did—I burst into tears.

"Bea. Bea. Are you safe? Are you at your apartment? Do you need the police? I can be there in—"

"I'm at The King's Land," I said.

"Are you okay?"

"Ronnie," I whispered like I was afraid to say it too loud, to chase away this feeling. "I think I'm happy. And I'm so scared I'll mess it up."

"Okay," she said, sounding somehow even more alarmed. "I'll be there in an hour. Two max."

"No. No. I don't want you to come. I don't need you."

Her silence was telling, and it seemed for that moment that something snapped between us. It wasn't painful. And it wasn't sad. Whatever broke wasn't needed anymore. A training wheel that was finally getting taken off.

"Why do you think you're going to ruin it?" she asked carefully.

"Because, isn't that what I do?"

"No. Honey. You don't ruin it. You just...don't expect enough from it."

I swallowed. "Expecting more seems like I'm asking to be disappointed. Expecting more—" I stopped.

"Seems like something you shouldn't have?" she asked.

"Yeah," I said, because she couldn't see me nod.

"What have I been telling you your whole life?" she whispered.

"That I deserve more."

"Yeah. And Mom used to tell me the same thing and she made me believe it. After she died I tried to do the same thing for you, but Dad and the Stepwitch were just so much louder than me."

"I deserve more," I said.

"And you're not going to mess it up."

It wasn't like a light switch got turned on and I suddenly believed this shit. But a light switch got turned on and I wanted to believe it.

And maybe that was the first step.

"Can you come this weekend?" I asked.

"Of course. We were having dinner at Sabrina's—"

"I'm going to be there, too," I said. Reinviting myself. Poor Cody was going to get a King Family Extravaganza.

"Really!" Her joy was so pure. So real.

"Yep. And I'm bringing a date."

"Holy shit...is my sister falling in love?"

"I don't know, Ronnie," I whispered because, again, I didn't want to startle this feeling away. "I just know I'm happy. Really happy."

Once Ronnie and I hung up I headed back up the stairs and down the hall toward the closed door of my room. Earlier, I'd skipped my old bedroom for Ronnie's simpler place. She'd let our stepmother paint her walls and dictate what she could put on the shelves until there was no real sign of Ronnie in her own bedroom.

It hadn't seemed to matter to Ronnie when all of it mattered to me. I'd fought every fight that came my way. Losing most of them hadn't slowed me down at all.

The gold doorknob was cool in my sticky hand and I had that kind of full-body memory of every single time I'd slammed this door. A million. I turned it and pushed it open, and as it always did, it got stuck a little on the carpet. My room was the same as it had been when I was teenager trying to figure my shit out.

The four-poster used to have pink and white fabric wrapped around it and I'd torn it down and replaced it with black and silver. I'd painted the walls a midnight blue and covered them with Nine Inch Nails posters. All my books were romance novels and erotica. No math trophies for me.

I had a dressing table with a mirror and...yep, in the second drawer down was the My Little Pony pencil case with a fifteen-year-old stash of weed.

The dogs started up the stairs, their tags jangling at different rhythms. Louise came in first and Thelma pushed the door open further with her body. There were face licks and some very investigative smelling of my body.

"Go," I muttered, giving them a push. "Get." They jumped onto the bed and curled up against the bare mattress together like they did at home.

My body still smelled like Cody and sex and I liked it.

"Bea?"

I closed my eyes at the sound of his voice, but I straightened my spine, too. Part of me was still braced to be hurt. For one of us to fuck this up. To get it wrong.

"In here!" I cried and I heard his step coming down the hallway until he stood in the doorway of my room. He'd pulled on his jeans but nothing else, and my mouth went dry and my body went wet at the sight of that lovely chest. Those bare feet. The rumpled hair.

His smile.

"You had a real vibe, huh?" he asked, taking in the dark splendor of my room.

"Goth wannabe," I said. "It made my stepmother crazy. That was reason enough to light the whole world on fire. "

Louise on the bed got up and growled at Cody.

"Holy shit, how did you get out of that porch?" he said.

"You put them in there?"

"The little one was cock-blocking me."

I laughed while Cody went over to the bare mattress and stood there while Louise sniffed him until she must have realized we smelled enough alike that he was acceptable.

He was quiet for a long time, like he was waiting for me to say something, and then I realized I was doing the same.

"What do we do now?" I asked.

"I feel like I still want to apologize."

"Me, too."

"I'm sorry," he said.

"I'm sorry," I said, and we smiled at each other.

"I'm gonna screw up again. I mean, I don't know when. And I'm not going to go seeking it out. But I feel like it's pretty inevitable."

"Yeah," he said. "I'm probably going to do the same."

"So?" I asked past the lump in my throat. "Do we shake hands? End it here—"

He cradled my face in his palms and kissed me so gently on the mouth. "No," he breathed across my lips. "That's not what I want."

"Me neither."

"You said...you said you were mine."

During sex. We'd been frantic saying that to each other. Like we needed to say it or die.

"You said I was yours."

"That's what I want," he said, kissing me again and then again. "That's all I want. For you to be mine and for me to be yours."

This sweetness was nearly unbearable. It was changing everything. The way I saw the world, the way I lived in my skin. It made anything seem possible.

Absolutely anything.

"Hey." I leaned into him. Pushing my belly against his until I felt his cock twitch.

"Yeah?"

"I need you to do something for me."

"Anything."

"I need you to fuck me in every room in this house so the dogs and I can live here."

He leaned back. "You're joking."

"I'm dead serious. I need good memories in this place, to replace the bad ones."

"Okay." He nodded solemnly. "How many rooms are we talking about here?"

"Including the bathrooms?"

"If you need me to fuck you in the bathroom, then I will fuck you in the bathroom."

"Fifteen rooms."

He smiled and then laughed, and then I was laughing, too. We held each other up as we howled and the dogs got into it, as well.

"Hey," he said, turning to shoo the dogs off the bed. They listened like he was another one of their humans and I felt my heart get too big in my chest. "You guys get. We better start if we're going to clear out a few of these rooms tonight."

He booted the dogs out the door and shut it behind them.

"You ready for this?" he asked, grinning at me. My broken-down cowboy with all the rules we shattered.

"So ready."

24

B

EA
Six months later

CODY WAS down at the barn. This was not a surprise. He was often down at the barn. It's where Bonnie was, and the dogs, and the two new horses he'd taken on this month. One was blind. The other was an ornery cuss.

Cody was a sucker for both of them.

"Hey," I said, walking between the stalls. "Cody?"

"Back here," he said, and I walked down the aisle carefully in my heels. This wasn't a formal dinner, but it was Christmas and it was a party. And...well, Cody liked me in heels. I turned the corner to see Cody in Bonnie's stall.

He wore his black suit that fit him like he was a superhero. Swear to God, that suit was probably going to get me pregnant one of these days.

"Am I late?" he asked. "I thought I had an hour—"

"You do.",

"Sabrina making you crazy?" he asked, grinning at me.

"Not at all. Jack on the other hand..."

"Well, he's in love. It's hard to blame him."

I was borrowing The Bar's chef for this party and Jack was supposed to be a guest but he couldn't quite keep that line clear. Cody and I had invited all our family—excluding his mother—Jack and the staff at The Bar, and a few other people around town. It was our first real shindig at the house.

Bonnie turned her head to rub her nose against me. A little head butt to the chest and I scratched her behind the ears. Louise, in the corner, farted and sighed. She'd taken up residence in Bonnie's stall about as easily as Cody and I had taken up residence in the house.

Which was to say, so easily.

Home like I never knew. And Cody worked some construction and he took in horses that needed love and I helped run The Bar and we were happy.

Which was to say, so happy.

"You nervous?" I asked, trying to keep my grin under control.

"Nah," he said.

"You shouldn't be," I said. "My brother is a normal guy."

"You Kings got a skewed idea of normal." Cody eyed me sideways but he was smiling. Dylan and Madison were coming in from Los Angeles for the party and staying with us at the ranch for a few days.

Cody was a little nervous.

I leaned over and kissed his mouth, right where his smile started.

"He puts his pants on one leg at a time," I whispered.

"Right before he kills people?" Cody asked.

"With his bare hands," I said, and we both laughed. I laughed a little harder than he did.

"Please don't be nervous. He's really a nice guy," I said. "And Maddie is super nice once you get to know her."

"Yeah, you said that about Clayton."

Clayton was taking the role of big brother to me very seriously. And it was sweet, but he had yet to warm up to Cody. Ronnie assured me it just took a little time and they needed to find some common ground. Which wasn't easy to locate between the self-made billionaire and the former rodeo star turned contractor.

Cody and Garret, Sabrina's husband, on the other hand, got along like a house on fire and suddenly Sabrina and I were double-dating. It was so weird.

"Charlie said he'd be a little late," Cody told me for the third time. His nerves were so sweet. His family meeting my family and all that stuff. "How are you not nervous?"

"I'm drunk."

"Bea!"

"Kidding. I'm not nervous because I love you, Cody." His face always went a little red when I said that. His ears got hot, like my words changed his chemistry for just a moment. Which made sense, because when he said it to me, I felt like I was floating. Like I was stoned on some powerful drug. "I love you so much. There's nothing to be nervous about when you're by my side."

He sighed and pressed his forehead to mine. Bonnie tried to nibble on his ear, but I saved him, wrapping my arms around his neck.

"I like this dress," he said, running his hand along all the sequins.

"I know you do."

"I like how it looks all crumpled up on the floor." I

laughed as his hand swept down over my ass. "I like how it looks bunched up around your waist."

"Yeah," I breathed. Getting hot under those silver sequins. And I'd come out here because he was nervous. And I had a little something on under this dress that would make him feel better. "I'm not so sure."

His chuckle was dark and dangerous and lit up every single thing inside my body.

"You need me to show you?" he breathed against my mouth. "You need me to show you how good you look with your dress up around your waist? Maybe I need to bend you over—"

His hand was pulling up my dress and I knew right away when he realized that what I had on under this dress was nothing.

"Bea," he groaned.

"You got about twenty minutes, cowboy. Make them count."

And that's the thing about my Cody. He made every single one of those minutes count.

EPILOGUE

B EA

THE WEDDING

Veronica burst into my big walk-in closet, slammed the door behind her, and lay back against it, as if the zombie hordes were on the other side. The dogs came in with her, panting at her side as if they'd been running for days instead of harassing Jack and Natalie for shrimp in the kitchen.

The dogs came over and sniffed me and then settled onto the couch in the corner.

Veronica, looking like an escapee from somewhere very glamorous, wore a glittery indigo evening dress and had three champagne glasses in one hand and a bottle of bubbly under one arm.

I wasn't sure which I was more excited about, the bubbly or my sister.

"I have déjà vu," Ronnie said, looking around. "Weren't we just here?"

"Seven years ago, and it was you in the dress." That had not ended happily, but I was in the business of turning bad memories in this house into good ones. Stellar ones, in fact. Beautiful, happy memories.

And so far, my record was flawless.

The ghosts in this dressing room didn't stand a chance against Cody and me.

"How are things going downstairs?" I asked.

"Natalie and Jack have things in hand," Ronnie said.

"Really?"

"Sure. Though I'm not sure if they're going screw each other on the canapes or throw them at each other."

That was kind of Jack and Natalie's dynamic. It was a good time.

I made to stand up from the stool of torture Sabrina currently had me positioned on, but Brina stopped me cold.

"Don't move," she said, barely an inch from my face. "You're going to be lopsided."

"Heaven forbid," I muttered, but settled back onto the stool. "It's your funeral," she muttered.

"Wedding, actually. But thanks."

Sabrina grinned at me and I grinned back. Because it was my wedding day and I was drunk on love. Love for my sisters. My brother. Champagne. Fake eyelashes. Even Jack and Natalie.   Cody.

I didn't care if I was lopsided and my caterers burned the house down.

Veronica popped the champagne and filled the three glasses, practically to the brim. Which made sense—it had been a rough three months for Veronica.

"What are you doing to her?" Veronica asked, leaning into my vision to see Sabrina's handiwork.

"Fake eyelashes."

"Why?"

"That's actually exactly what I'm asking myself," I said. I had agreed to let Sabrina do my makeup when I was drunk on very fine bourbon. And love. It had been a real love bender around here for the past few months.

"So, she will look doe-like," Sabrina said, and then finally stepped back. "Voila! What do you think?"

The stool I'd been sitting on was in the mirrored alcove where Veronica, seven years ago on the night of her engagement party, had stood and been ripped to shreds by our step-mom. I hadn't redecorated the room because I never used it, but Cody and I had banished all ghosts of unhappiness by fucking on pretty much every flat surface in the place.

It was outrageously effective.

I blinked at myself in the mirror. I wasn't in my dress yet, but my hair and makeup were done. I'd grown my hair out long and Sabrina had curled it into soft waves that fell, nice and inky, over my shoulders. And my makeup was perfect. It was me, totally me, but just a little softer. More romantic.

"See?" Sabrina said with a big grin. "Doe-like."

"What do you think?" I asked Ronnie, who was sprawled across the couch. Half her champagne gone. The dogs banished to the floor.

"You're beautiful," she said. "You're skinny. Your boobs are a normal size. Your vagina hasn't been ripped apart. Everything is roses for you right now, Bea. You better enjoy it."

"Are you sure you're supposed to be drinking?" Sabrina asked her, and Veronica shot lasers out of her eyes.

Sabrina lifted her hands in surrender and I was surprised she wasn't smoking.

"Later on tonight I'm going to lock myself in a bathroom and do something called pump and dump. Which sounds gross, but I'll be doing it. I've been stockpiling milk for weeks. Milking myself like a cow, which in case you're wondering, is in fact worse than it sounds in preparation for this night. So I could enjoy what would be basically the weight of my breasts in champagne. For one night. One." She leaned forward to scratch one of the dogs and her incredibly impressive breasts challenged the bodice of her gown. For a second, I was pretty sure the boobs would win. But then she leaned back against the couch. "And now everyone is giving me dirty looks for even holding a champagne glass and it's been a year! A year without a drop—"

Sabrina handed Ronnie her glass. "You need this more than me," she said, and Veronica took it. Shot it back without pausing.

"Thank you," Veronica said.

"Is it really that bad?"

"Yep."

"I'm going to take my breasts and my vagina and put on my dress," I said. Sabrina sat down next to Ronnie and the dogs came over to try and get in her lap. I loved how the dogs loved Sabrina and how she didn't love them back.

It was entertaining.

The dress was in the small dressing room, hanging off a hook. I'd gone with tight, full-length lace gown with a real Stevie Nicks vibe to it. And I was wiggling into it when I heard the dressing room door open again.

"Jesus Christ," my brother Dylan muttered. "I knew you'd be in here. You got room?"

I heard them all shifting on the couch, making room for Dylan's big, powerful frame.

"Where's Maddy?" Sabrina asked.

"She and Clayton are talking shop."

All three of them groaned.

"Is that bourbon?" Ronnie asked.

"Yeah. I brought...you want?... Okay, then."

I got the dress on and zipped as much as I could and told myself not to cry. That it was too early. That being drunk on love was no reason to spend most of the day in tears. I didn't want Cody to lift my veil and find me all red-faced and swollen-eyed.

But I stepped out into that mirrored area and saw them all squeezed onto that couch. My handsome brother in a tux, my beautiful sisters in the blue dresses they'd picked out—and the tears welled up again.

"No!" Sabrina cried, jumping up as if I'd started myself on fire. "Don't you dare start crying."

"I'm just so happy."

She pinched me.

"Ow!" I cried and smacked her hand away. Ronnie, now holding a glass of bourbon, leaned back on that couch and laughed and laughed.

"Stopped you from crying," Sabrina said.

Dylan, looking like a deadly million bucks, unfolded his long legs and walked to stand in front of me. My brother. The guy I'd idolized and hero-worshipped.

When I'd asked him to walk me down the aisle, he'd needed a second to get himself together before telling me yes. Of course.

"Look at you," he breathed and I felt the burning in my eyes. "Who would have guessed you'd clean up so nice?"

"Oh my god!" I cried and smacked him.

"Seriously, I half expected you to walk down the aisle in cutoffs," he said.

"With hay in your hair," Ronnie chimed in from the couch, lifting that glass of bourbon as if in a toast.

"She hasn't had a drink in a year," I breathed to Sabrina. "And she was always kind of a lightweight."

"On it," she said, leaving me with Dylan for a second in front of the mirrors to handle my determined-to-get-drunk sister.

We looked, oddly, the most alike. Dylan and I. Of all the Kings. Versions of our father, which I knew caused both of us some trouble over the years. Looking in the mirror and seeing the man who hurt us both so bad. It gave us some rough moments. "Seriously," Dylan said, "you're beautiful. And I'm so proud to be walking you down that aisle."

"You're going to make me cry."

"Here," he said and turned to the small table. "I brought you some bourbon. The good stuff." There was a bottle and four glasses, crowded in with the champagne and the three flutes. I took the bourbon he handed me and had a sip. I was a crier when I had too much to drink, so I kept it to a sip.

But it was the really, really good stuff.

"Come on," Sabrina said. "Let's put on the flowers."

The florist had made a beautiful crown of wildflowers, mostly forget-me-nots and bluebells. Sabrina pulled it from the box and placed it on my head, arranging the curls just so.

"Oh my god," Ronnie said, getting up off the couch to hug me. "You're stunning. You're absolutely beautiful."

I turned to look at myself in the mirror, flanked by my siblings. I thought of how far we'd come. The years of distrust and dislike, fuelled by our father. It was a miracle we got here. To friendship. To family.

"I love you," I breathed.

"You're drunk," Ronnie said and we all laughed.

"No. I'm not... I mean... drunk on love, yes. But if I can't tell you all that I love you on my wedding day, when can I?"

"Well," Dylan said, with that charming sly grin. "You can tell me anytime. Sabrina might have rules about that sort of thing—"

"Stop." Sabrina swatted him.

"We love you too, Bea," Ronnie whispered and kissed my cheek. It took us too long to get here, but it only made being here so sweet. So impossibly sweet.

"What's...that smell?" Sabrina asked, and we all started sniffing.

"It's you!" Sabrina said and pointed to Ronnie. "It's that."

On the sparkly bodice of her gown there was a small bit of dried liquid.

"Spit-up," Ronnie said. "It's spit-up. Of course it is. Because that's my life now, you know?"

"Oh my god, further proof Maddy and I have made the right decision," Dylan said and sat back down on the couch while Sabrina and Ronnie tried to wipe off the spit-up. "No spit-up. Nothing but sex and spontaneous vacations and—"

"You're not helping," I muttered.

"Have I mentioned the sleep? So much sleep."

"Fuck off, Dylan. Seriously," Ronnie said. But she was laughing. Or crying? Hard to say.

"I don't know why you want to rub it in," I said.

"It's too late for Ronnie. But you and Sabrina?" He shrugged. "I might still be able to save you."

"Actually," Sabrina said, but was interrupted by another knock on the door.

"If that's my baby, I'm not here," Ronnie said, and Sabrina gasped. Horrified. Missing the joke entirely. Ronnie waved her off.

"Hey." Garrett poked his head around the door, looking like a handsome devil in a dark suit. "Look at you," he breathed, coming in and shutting the door behind him.

"It's your wife's good work," I said, putting my arm around Sabrina.

"I was actually talking to Sabrina. But you're not bad either," he said with a wink and then leaned in to kiss me.

"Don't mess up the flowers," Sabrina said.

Garrett and I shared a laughing look. "Honestly, Bea. You look stunning," he said.

"Thank you."

"Drink?" Dylan asked. "We have champagne and bourbon."

"Together?" Garrett asked. "Sounds like one of Bea's creations."

"You can try that, but I'm serving them separately," Dylan said.

"Bourbon," Garrett said, and Dylan handed him the rocks glass with an inch of booze in it. "So?" Garrett said to Sabrina, all bright-eyed and smiling. Like a man sitting on good news. "Did you tell them?"

"I was just about to," Sabrina said and then smiled at all of us, running her hand down her flat belly. It took a second for the penny to drop, but when it did—it really did.

"No shit!" I cried.

"No shit!" Veronica cried.

"Oh shit," Dylan muttered.

But all three of us wrapped her in our arms.

"I'm sorry," Sabrina said to me. "I didn't want to take the

attention on your wedding day, but we figured people were going to ask if I wasn't drinking."

"Are you kidding?" I asked. "I'm so thrilled you told us. Today or any day."

"Thanks, sis," she said.

Veronica launched into a litany of questions about sleep and morning sickness.

Dylan reached out and shook Garrett's hand. "Congratulations, man," he said. "A few more guys like you in the world isn't a bad thing."

"Or women like her," Garrett said, looking at his wife with so much love on his face I nearly started crying again.

"Don't you start," Sabrina warned me. "Or I'll pinch you again."

I was saved by another knock on the door.

"Come in," we all said and Clayton pushed open the door.

His three-month-old son was cradled in his arms, sleeping like there would never be a safer place for him in this world.

Maddy was behind him, wearing another indigo dress, cut close to her body. Her honey blonde hair as smooth as silk.

"There you are," Maddy said, smiling at her husband, Dylan. He brightened when he saw her. She slipped in beside Dylan like that spot at his side had been made for her. He lifted one of the rocks glasses and handed it to her. "I saw you coming up here with the good stuff."

"I was trying to have a drink with my sisters."

"And it turned into a party?" Maddy asked.

"It usually does," Dylan said.

"How are you guys doing?" Ronnie asked, leaning over Clayton's arms to peek at the sleeping Matthew.

"So good," Clayton said and then kissed her so sweetly on the lips. They shared a look of such warmth, such comfort that the whole room sucked in a breath. My imperious brother-in-law, the cutthroat businessman, was an absolute fool for my sister and his son.

It was about the most beautiful thing I'd ever seen.

Dylan handed a glass of champagne to Clayton.

"A toast?" Maddy asked.

"To the bride," Clayton said.

I shook my head and lifted my own glass of bourbon. "To us. To the Kings. To happily ever afters. And new generations." I looked at my beautiful nephew, and Sabrina with the tiny life growing in her stomach.

God, I could not stand to be this happy. It didn't seem sustainable.

Sabrina pinched me again.

"Doesn't seem right to do this without Cody," Garrett said. "He's a King, too."

"Not yet," Dylan said.

"Let's go change that," I said and shot back the last of my bourbon. And then I led my family out of that dressing room down to the party below and the future that waited for me.

Cody.

It was time to complete my family with the man I loved.

Is this your first King Family book? Well, lucky for you there are three more!

The Tycoon Veronica's story

The Bodyguard Sabrina's story

The Bastard Dylan's story

. . .

ARE you ready for Jack's story? It will be an exclusive audio book in the Read Me Romance Podcast. To find out when it will be released - join my newsletter.

HAVE you read THE DEBT series? Turn the page for an excerpt of the first book Bad Neighbor.

25

EXCERPT OF BAD NEIGHBOR

hapter 1

IN THE END the futon was my downfall.

It wasn't having my sister leave for parts unknown.

Or giving her most of my money.

Or moving out of the condo I loved so much, only to move to this shit hole apartment, where there was a good chance I was going to get knifed before I even got my stuff in the door.

So far, none of that had made me so much as swear. Much less cry. Or scream.

That stuff is just my life. It's the shit that happens to me. Part of being a twin to my sister.

But this futon...

This futon is a punishment from God. It is the universe laughing at me.

It was stuck in the door of my new apartment, folded up like a taco. An immoveable three thousand pound taco.

And it wasn't moving.

This is just what you get for not hiring movers. Or having a boyfriend. Or anyone really, who could help move a girl with five boxes, three garbage bags and a futon mattress to her name.

Oh and several thousand dollars in computer and drafting equipment. All sitting safely in the corner of my apartment. I moved Izzy in first (yes, I named my system. It seemed only right, considering how much time I spend with her) and threw a sheet over her. Paranoid about this new neighborhood I locked up between trips to my rental truck to get the rest of my stuff. Which was now all sitting behind me on the cracked cement walk way.

Except for the current bane of my existence.

The futon.

Which, I'd like to point out, I got out of the back of the truck, dragged down the path from the parking garage to this point, actually folded it up like a taco and got it halfway through the door.

But now my shaky-exhausted-unused-to-this-amount-of-work (any kind of work actually that doesn't involve a mouse, a pencil or a stylus) muscles have given up.

And to add insult to injury, my hair was getting in on the joke, by pulling out of my hair elastic and head band to pop up in white blond corkscrews and fall into my face. It was sticking to my neck.

It was making me crazy.

Everything. Every single thing was making me crazy. After two weeks of keeping my shit together I was going to lose it. Right here.

Stop. Charlotte, you can do this.

I gave myself a little pep talk and swallowed down the primal scream of "WHAT THE FUCK HAS HAPPENED TO MY LIFE!"

"Come on," I muttered and put my back up against the futon. I put my back against it and pushed. And got nothing. Got nowhere.

Exhausted, my legs buckled and I barely caught myself against the futon before landing flat on my butt.

I turned and pushed my face and hands against the futon stretched my legs out behind me and pushed with all my not inconsiderable weight.

Suddenly, it bent sideways, throwing me nearly into the wall and then lodged itself, half in my door and half against the metal staircase leading up to the second floor of the apartment building.

Nope. No. I wasn't going to cry. Not over this.

I just needed help.

And if the thought of actually having to talk to a human to make that help happen, seemed to me to be worse than the futon nightmare, that was just my damage.

You have to get over this, my sister used to tell me. The world is full of people. No one lives a completely people-free life.

The only people I used to need were my sister, the girl who made my afternoon coffee at the coffee shop on my old corner and the fantasy of one of the guys down at the organic fruit stand where I used to live.

But now they were all gone.

I needed new people.

And the fact that I had to find those people here, at Shady Oaks, this end of the road place... well, it made me want to howl.

The small outdoor courtyard I was currently trapped in

was empty. The three stories of balcony loomed over my head, the chipped paint a kind of non-descript beige. The pool in the middle filled with a half-foot of last year's dried up leaves and a few hundred cigarette buts, had a few busted up lawn chairs sitting around it's edge, but no one was sitting in them. The laundry area beneath the staircase directly across the courtyard from me was dark and quiet

My new apartment was beneath the other corner stairway, a weird little shadowy enclave of privacy that the superintendent said leaked but only when it rained.

The superintendent was more funny sob, than funny ha ha, if you asked me.

I'd never actually met the super, if you could believe that. Everything was done through email. Which at the time had seemed ideal. Now it seemed...sketchy.

Shady Oaks was a ghost town.

Normally I'd love that. But today, today I just needed a little help. Today I needed a flesh and blood person.

And of course there was no one.

I gave myself exactly a three count of pity. That was it. That was all I got.

One.

Two.

"What's going on?" a voice asked. A male voice. And I leaned away from the wall and looked around my futon mattress to see a ... guy.

Like a guy guy. A hot guy.

A man, really.

A very sweaty man. His frayed grey tee shirt where it stretched across his shoulders was black with sweat and it poured down his face. He was my height, maybe a few inches taller. Which in the world of dudes made him kind of short. But he was thick and square, giving the impression that he was taller then he was. And bigger.

Did I say big?

While I watched he lifted the bottom edge of his shirt and wiped his forehead, revealing that even his six-pack abs were sweating.

"You gonna move this thing?" he asked, scowling at me while I stared at his abs.

I blew a curl out of my face and tried for my best cheerful tone. I even smiled.

"Trying to. But I think the futon likes it here."

"I can't get into my apartment." Ignoring my joke, he pointed at the door next to mine, the door he couldn't get to past the futon barricade.

"Oh," I said, inanely, trying not to stare at his sweat or his body. "We're neighbors."

"Yeah. What are you doing with the futon?"

"Well, you're welcome to try and reason with it, but I've found it very disagreeable-"

"You moving it in or out?" he asked. My charm completely not charming to him.

"In-"

With one hand - *one hand* - he shoved the futon into my apartment. After it squeezed through the door it flopped open in the middle of my white tiled kitchen.

I leaned into my doorway.

"Wow." Was all I could say.

"You want it there?" he asked.

"In my kitchen?" I laughed. "While I can appreciate the commute for coffee-"

Sweaty grumpy guy had dark brown eyes - pantone color 0937 TCX, if I was being exact - set wide in a flushed face and I only got a glimpse of them before he was inside my apartment.

Without asking, he just stomped right in.

"Wait...what?"

"Bedroom?" he asked.

I blinked at him, thinking of my livelihood under the sheet in the corner and if he tried to rob me I wouldn't be able to stop him.

I wouldn't be able to stop him from doing...anything.

And I'd had that fantasy about the guys at the fruit stand locking me inside the store with all of them. But this was not that.

This was Shady Oaks and a burly stranger just walking into my apartment like he had that kind of right.

"Do you want this in your bedroom?" He said it slowly like I was an idiot.

"You don't have to do this."

"You can't do it." His eyes skated across my body, taking in my paint-splattered overalls and the hot pink tank top I wore underneath it.

He couldn't see that my tank top had Big Bird on it. But he looked at me like he knew.

He looked at me like I had a sign that said 185 pound weakling on it.

"I'm putting it in your bedroom."

And he took the futon by the corner, like the hand of a misbehaving child, and dragged it through my shabby kitchen past the living room with it's bank of barred windows and then into my bedroom. I followed but stopped in the living room by the sheet-covered Izzy, as if to keep her calm, or to stand in his way in case he tried to touch her.

I could just see the shadow of him in my bedroom as he all but tossed my futon onto the floor.

Funny how he was doing a nice thing but still I managed to feel both threatened and insulted.

Deep breath, Charlotte, I told myself. *Deep breath.*

He was out a second later, standing in the doorway of my bedroom, thick and square. His damp shirt clung to every muscle. And he had...he had a lot of muscles. Thick round knobs of them. Lean, hard planes of them. He was made of muscles.

He'd been running, or working out or something. He wore running shoes and athletic shorts that were frayed in the same well-used way his shirt was. White earbuds had been tucked into the waistband of his shorts, and dangled down by his...well. Shorts.

His black hair was buzzcut short, down practically to his scalp. And his face, now that the flush was gone and the sweat had slowed down, looked like it had recently taken a beating. His eye was dark and his lip had a cut. His nose looked like it had been broken a few times.

He carried himself like a guy who lived in his whole body. Like every molecule was under his control. I lived in exactly 12% of my body. I wasn't even sure what my hair was doing.

"You done?" he asked.

"Moving-"

"Staring."

All the blood in my body roared to my face. My stomach curled into a ball like a wounded hedgehog trying to protect itself from further harm.

"Thank you," I said, staring intently at the edge of a tile in my kitchen. It was chipped, the white enamel long gone. "That was nice of you to help."

"No big deal." He stepped into the living room and I

went back against the wall giving him a wide wide berth. Wanting to keep as much distance between us as I could.

He stopped. "What are you doing?"

"Nothing."

"You think I'm going to hurt you?"

"I'm not sure what you're going to do."

He made a grunting noise and stood there like he was waiting for me to look at him, but I did not. I burned under his gaze and fussed with my sheet, wishing Izzy was set up so I could just work, instead of... this.

Instead of being human with humans.

And then he was gone. Leaving behind the smell of man. And sweat. And it was not a bad smell. It was just different and it did not belong in my space.

I folded forward at the waist, sucking in a breath.

Jeez. Wow.

That dude was potent.

And I was pretty much an idiot.

I walked into the bedroom and used all of my strength to slide the futon out of the middle of the room and against the wall. There was another thump in the living room and I realized with my heart in my throat that I'd left my door open. I ran out only to find my sheet still over Izzy but the rest of my stuff had been brought in.

Two big boxes and the garbage bags.

He'd moved the rest of my stuff in and then he left.

That was...nice.

Unexpected and nice.

Neighborly, even.

I thought about knocking on his door to say thank you. It's what I should do. It was the right thing to do. Neighborly. It was what my sister would have done.

My sister would have gone over and thanked him and then probably screwed him.

But I was not that person. I was the opposite of that person.

Silently, like he could hear me and maybe he could, I had no idea how thick these walls were, I stepped to my door and then shut it.

And then locked it.

And chained it.

Taking a deep breath I turned and looked at my new home, with it's chipped tile and the barred windows. The bare lightbulbs hanging from the ceiling. Outside there was a siren and a dog barking.

Next door my neighbor turned on his stereo answering the question regarding how thick my walls were. Paper thin.

For a moment the grief and the panic and fear were overwhelming. Tears burned behind my eyes and I couldn't take a deep breath. But I pushed the panic back. Smothered it. Just set it aside like a bag I didn't want to carry anymore. I had so many of those kinds of bags, all along the edges of my life.

I closed my eyes and searched for calm.

Deep breath, Charlotte. This is not so bad. This is not forever. This is not permanent. This place is not your world.

I opened my eyes and took in my new home again; with my rose-colored glasses fully in place.

It wasn't so bad here. The hard wood floors in the living room and bedroom were nice. A coat of paint. Some curtains to hide the bars. My coffee pot. Izzy up and humming in the corner.

It would feel like home. It would.

I could ignore the neighbor. I was good at ignoring actual humans.

As bad as this place was, and it was bad, I had to remind myself that it was actually perfect.

Because no one – even if they were looking – would find me here.

And my sister was okay. She was safe.

Which was all that mattered.

GET YOUR COPY HERE